PENGUIN BOOKS
"WHAT WOULD YOU DO TO SAVE
THE WORLD?"

Ira Trivedi has lived in nine different cities, across four countries
and three continents. She has studied Economics and
International Relations at Wellesley College, and been a student
of French in Aix-en-Provence in the South of France. She took
part in the *Femina* Miss India contest in 2004.

"What Would You Do to Save the World?"

confessions of a could-have-been beauty queen

IRA TRIVEDI

PENGUIN BOOKS

PENGUIN BOOKS
Published by the Penguin Group
Penguin Books India Pvt Ltd, 11 Community Centre, Panchsheel Park,
New Delhi 110 017, India
Penguin Group (USA) Inc., 375 Hudson Street, New York, New York
10014, USA
Penguin Group (Canada), 90 Eglinton Avenue East, Suite 700, Toronto,
Ontario, M4P 2Y3, Canada (a division of Pearson Penguin Canada Inc.)
Penguin Books Ltd, 80 Strand, London WC2R 0RL, England
Penguin Ireland, 25 St Stephen's Green, Dublin 2, Ireland (a division of
Penguin Books Ltd)
Penguin Group (Australia), 250 Camberwell Road, Camberwell, Victoria
3124, Australia (a division of Pearson Australia Group Pty Ltd)
Penguin Group (NZ), cnr Airborne and Rosedale Roads, Albany,
Auckland 1310, New Zealand (a division of Pearson New Zealand Ltd)
Penguin Group (South Africa) (Pty) Ltd, 24 Sturdee Avenue, Rosebank,
Johannesburg 2196, South Africa

Penguin Books Ltd, Registered Offices: 80 Strand, London WC2R 0RL,
England

First published by Penguin Books India 2006

ISBN-13: 978-0-14400-143-9 ISBN-10: 0-14400-143-8

This is a work of fiction. Names, characters, places and incidents are
either the product of the author's imagination or are used fictitiously and
any resemblance to any actual person, living or dead, events or locales is
entirely coincidental.

Typeset in Perpetua by Mantra Virtual Services, New Delhi
Printed at Baba Barkhanath Printers, New Delhi

For my parents.
Because you are everything.

Contents

Welcome to the world of beauty. A world of magnificence and splendour, a world of fluff and powder. A world shaded in hues of pink and white, cast in gentleness and warmth; a world so delicate, that it might just disappear on a touch. Welcome to the world of plastic, where things are not what they appear to be, where behind the glitter and lights there is darkness, behind the diamonds there is dust, and behind the smiles there are tears. This is the world that I entered and attempted to conquer, but fell—fell hard on to the impliable bed of reality.

I thought that the Miss Indian Beauty contest was only a beauty pageant. I was wrong. It goes much, much deeper than that. It was the hope for so many Indian girls, from the small-town girl in Bihar to the new-age Indian woman from Mumbai, the jet-setting NRI from New Zealand to the little girl who watched the pageant glued to her TV set. So many little girls held the hope, deep in their hearts, of being Miss Indian Beauty someday. This is my story, and also the story of twenty-three such girls who came together, each one of them vying for the crown.

Each one of us had put our lives on hold to pursue our dream of being Miss Indian Beauty. In these pages I present to you the story as seen from my eyes. A naive, stubborn and spirited girl who was an outsider on the inside, who went out there to conquer the world, and though she may have lost the crown, won a whole lot more.

Presenting the one and only . . .

This wasn't just *any old* beauty pageant. This was *the* Miss Indian Beauty contest—the pageant to top all beauty pageants, a ticket to instant fame and success. Over the past twenty years it had established itself as an institution— an institution that could thrust an average small-town girl into the limelight, and even be a direct, overnight, first A.C. ticket into Bollywood. When I think about it now, analytically, strategically, in a completely sane fashion, after the sparkling crowning ceremony has taken place, in the aftermath of it all, I still haven't been able to figure out what drove me to take part. I had entered a state of temporary insanity, where the little girl in me, the one who had cut out the glossy Miss Indian Beauty entry forms from the women's magazines that came home every month, had broken through the layers of age and wisdom, put on her mother's high heels and wobbled down the ramp. The

Miss Indian Beauty contest had been my secret dream, the trump card that I would play to turn my monochrome life into a technicolour dream.

Why now? Why now, when I was probably happier than I had ever been before? I had struggled through school in Indore, gone through the gruelling board exam experience, struggled with college applications and finally gotten into college. I was past the days of teenage languor, the days of infatuation, staring at the phone waiting for it to ring, the days of all-night MSN chatting and phone conversations. I was in a reputable college, doing well in my classes, and had a cute boyfriend. Things were stable.

I think this 'stable' state is what scared the shit out of me. I was scared of leading an 'ordinary life'. I envisioned the future I was heading towards. I would graduate from Wellesley College, work on Wall Street, get married to a loving doctor or lawyer, have a few kids, be happy driving my SUV and innovating in the kitchen.

I wanted to be a star, and Miss Indian Beauty was the key.

I had no training, no background, I had never walked down a ramp, or even been in front of the camera. Hell, I wasn't even adept at the simple tasks of blow-drying my hair or applying eyeliner. But you see, that was the charm of the Miss Indian Beauty pageant. Much like a Bollywood movie, it idealized escapism. The history of the Miss Indian Beauty pageant is replete with tales and stories, legends in

2

which young, simple, small-town girls are crowned with diamonds, dressed in silk, and taken through a magical journey towards success and fame.

In my deepest, darkest fantasies, I too wanted to be part of an absurd dance sequence and thrust in tune with the music. I too wanted to put on glittery, racy outfits and be the star of the show. The little girl in me had wanted to pull out the ribbons in my plaited hair, kick off the dusty Bata school shoes and put on a princess dress. The big girl in me wanted to dress in Dolce and Gabbana, wear Manolos, and be the life of the party.

I figured I had the basics. A decent face (very ordinary to some, but stunningly beautiful to others), the brains (enough to answer random questions anyway), and most importantly, the height (a très important quality that I will explain in detail). But I never asked myself the most important question, because I figured the answer was obvious. I never once questioned myself about whether I had the capability to really do this. I never asked myself if I would actually enjoy the camera, walking down the ramp, being the crowned princess, and being bestowed a title that would be attached to my name for a lifetime. It was a dream, more of a fantasy, rather. But sometimes fantasies are enjoyed best when they remain fantasies.

How would I describe myself? Even though I have a practiced beauty pageant answer for this question, when I try to put it down on paper, it's tough. I would say I am

3

struggling—struggling hard, just to be above average. It is so easy, so simple to end up ordinary. I wanted to be a cut above the rest. What I didn't realize was, so does the rest of the world.

Mumbai is a divided city. From Nariman Point to Worli exists the world of South Bombay, and anything further than Worli is referred to as the 'suburbs' and looked upon with disdain by the smug inhabitants of South Bombay. On one side of this divide lives the old money of Mumbai. In their high-rise buildings, moist with age, these people have earned their money the old-fashioned way—they've inherited it. On the other side live the nouveau riche, in their spanking new seaside bungalows. There is a name for this division, and that name is 'filmi'. The suburbs are synonymous with the movie industry and the film stars. One can actually feel the difference on either side of the divide. On one side, tall grim buildings rise up as high as the eye can see, and inside these buildings, in hardwood conference rooms, lies the heart of corporate India. The gravity of the goings-on inside these buildings hangs in the air. South Bombay is enveloped in a solitary, serious calm. On the other side of the divide, the easy, wistful world of Bollywood and its sheer razzmatazz seeps into the rowdy streets where the beautiful people live.

My college boyfriend Rushab was your typical South Bombay boy. Born and brought up in Breach Candy, he was sent off to Switzerland for school, and then to Boston for college, after which he returned to the homeland where he was now preparing to take over his father's business. He was a true South Bombay boy, in that he believed that the world that he lived in was the only one that existed.

How do you tell your boyfriend, someone who refused to even take a step past the dividing line between South Bombay and the suburbs, that you were—of all things— entering a beauty contest? Well, cocktails help, but don't necessarily solve the problem. I had a feeling that Rushab already had an inkling of my Miss Indian Beauty aspirations. He knew that taking part in the Miss Indian Beauty pageant was a fantasy that I meant to pursue someday, and that I might possibly be crazy enough to even go through with it. Little did he realize that this day was approaching so quickly.

That night is vividly clear in my mind. I remember us lounging at the Opium Den, a bar at the Oberoi, sipping on substandard apple martinis, when I hesitantly broke the news to him. 'Rushab, baby, I have something important to tell you.' His face immediately became serious on hearing my tone of voice. 'What's up?'

'Listen, darling . . . I'm on the verge of doing something big . . . I'm going to enter the Miss Indian Beauty contest!' I remember the look of growing horror on his face as I proceeded to tell him the details. 'Holy shit, Riya!'

He was pissed. He never called me by my name, it was always 'honey', 'pookie' or 'baby'. 'Listen Riya, girls like you, khandani girls like you, girls from well-respected homes and families, girls who go to good schools and have done real things—they just don't do this type of thing!' This hit hard at the lump of inhibition that lay inside me, and in a spate of fury I spat out, 'Rushab, you don't know anything. Isn't it ironic that all the girls who win this contest end up eventually marrying the men who come from these so-called khandani families? Things have changed, babe. Don't be a dork.' I spewed out a list of Miss Indian Beauties who had charmed and married men from immensely wealthy, typically khandani families.

Rushab didn't say anything more to me. He knew that my stubborn side had decided to go through with this, and that there was no stopping me. Also, I knew that underneath that frozen mask of horror lay curiosity, and just a teensy-weensy bit of excitement. His girlfriend was going to be on TV!

That night as I lay in bed, unable to sleep, I realized that he had a point. What kind of girl typically runs for a beauty pageant? Someone who did not have too much to lose, but a whole lot to win. These contests were for girls for whom the crown would create a life, and who in return would dedicate their lives to the crown. Was this really what I wanted? Was I ready to be classified as a Miss Indian Beauty girl? Rushab's point, like a razor-sharp knife, would prick at me at regular intervals throughout the course of the pageant.

Breaking the news to Rushab was a mere test run. The parents would be much tougher to tackle. Tonight was the night. I took a deep breath and went down to the dinner table, where my mother and father sat waiting for me. My special meal of soup and non-fried subzi had been set at the table. I sat down and began, 'Daddy and Mom, I have something to tell you guys.'

Between bites of aloo-gobi, my mom nodded her head. I wasn't sure if this was the right time—she looked somewhat distracted by the dal, which was a strange colour tonight. Dad looked deeply engrossed in his meal. I took a deep breath and began.

'Dad, you know that I have always wanted to run for the Miss Indian Beauty pageant.' There was silence. 'Well, I think I am ready to do it.' Mom looked up from the dal, and my father spilled his soup. They seemed alarmed, though thankfully not completely shocked. My mom kept silent and just looked at my dad. This was standard practice when something of importance was being discussed. I was relieved to see the she didn't look angry, maybe even a tad bit excited. My father had a habit of rubbing this one spot on his head when he was doing some heavy thinking. He rubbed it at length until he finally responded, 'Achaa . . . what about college then?' 'Well,' I said, trying to appear nonchalant. 'I think I am going to take a semester off . . . it's not a big deal—in fact, our dean encourages it.' 'I see,' said my father as he continued to rub the balding spot. 'Chalo . . . God's grace . . . ,' said my mom. She brought God into everything. 'So, are you prepared for it, wardrobe and all?' That was a statement of approval. 'You know, Premlata aunty has started making some really nice Western stuff.' I interrupted my mom. 'Hm,' I said. I didn't want to encourage her on this.

And so the secret was revealed to my parents. It's not that they were wholly opposed to the idea of me taking part in a beauty pageant. I mean, it was going against the very Brahmin academic tradition of the family, but at the same time it was a little exciting too. But I could tell that it was scary for them that their daughter was about to enter an alien world. What would happen if I won the coveted title? Would it mar my prospects of finding a 'good' husband? As I approached a 'marriageable age', they were extra-sensitive to the potential stigma attached to the title of a beauty queen.

I talked to my parents late into the night. Why did I want to win this crown? Since Bollywood was definitely not the path that I wanted to follow, where would this title lead me? I really had no concrete idea of what I would do with the title. Hell, if anything, it would look pretty damn cool on a resume. I just knew that it would give me a golden halo. It would elevate me above the ordinary, and at this point what scared me most was being just another face in the crowd.

8

Hidden hopes

I decided to pursue my Miss Indian Beauty hopes actively, in an attempt to transform my fantasy into reality. For the next six months, my decision was an invisible force that kept me going. I remained in the closet about my ambition. I could not bear the idea of telling people that I was in the running for, of all things, a beauty pageant. I was afraid people would think that I was pretentious, pompous and arrogant. I mean really—running for a beauty pageant wasn't really the most reputable thing to do. I never, ever wanted people to think of me as Miss Indian Beauty wannabe, so I kept my aspirations under complete wraps. I continued to lead my ordinary life, and spent the days conjuring up dreams cast in the world of glamour, losing myself on many an occasion in the warmth and fullness of these hollow yet glittery thoughts. This same desire gave me the strength to go on a hardcore diet, and I soon lost all those kilos I had gained from late-night studying and junk food sessions in college. Through the exercise of great self-control, I am proud to say that I lost a total of six kilos in three months, to reach an all-time low of fifty-two kilograms (not bad when you are 5' 9").

The months went by, and I kept my secret to myself. I eagerly awaited the day I would carefully cut the entry form along the dotted lines, filling it out in bold, black ink. I would enclose it in a manila envelope, spray a dash of perfume to ensure a pleasant evaluation, and kiss the package adieu, in hopes of a diamond crown.

The application required photographs to be submitted along with the entry form. That too not just ordinary photographs, but 'portfolio photos'. I was in Bhopal, Madhya Pradesh, where my father had been posted for the last two years. There is something to be said about the drowsy atmosphere that exists in Bhopal, and I was pleased to be back home after a rather strenuous semester, sipping chai, basking in my dream world of diamonds, imagining my moment of victory. Now that the time had come to take the first tangible step towards my goal, I was nervous and, to a certain point, hesitant to go through with this. I would have to make a trip to hectic, crazy Mumbai, dish out Rs 20,000, and undergo the process of a portfolio shoot. I'd never been through the experience, but I guessed that it could be quite excruciating—I felt uncomfortable enough posing for a passport photograph.

But I had to get a portfolio together, and in a rather nervous attempt to get it done, I contacted our family photographer, Mr Agni, the owner of a small-time Kodak photo studio in Indore to take on the job. I had never met Mr Agni before, but knew that he loved to send his daughter's sindhi cooking home to us. In the array of sindhi curries, subzis and chutneys that came our way there was always the special treat of sindhi halwa, floating in a generous pool of ghee replete with dry fruits that he would send especially for me. I would praise his daughter's cooking so profusely each time the halwa came my way that he had developed a special liking for my glorific ways, and was thrilled when he was assigned this task. Not surprisingly, he assumed that the intention of this photo shoot was matrimony, and immediately sent across some more halwa for me. Definitely not the most conducive thing for a beauty-queen diet.

It was a four-hour drive to Indore, and I took with me five outfits that I thought looked quite nice. I found a local beautician, Juhi (who liked to be called 'Jewels'), for make-up and hair. When I told her that I was getting on ways to a photo shoot, she immediately broke into marriage talk, giving me the lowdown on the best jewellers and hennawalis in town. Apparently this was standard procedure. Throughout the course of the session, I emphasized that I wanted *light* make-up. I suspected Jewels could have a tendency to go a bit crazy with the blues and the pinks, trying to recreate the 'glam-doll' make-up ads that she saw in the glossy magazines that came to her salon. Little did she realize that the pinks and blues went rather well with blonde hair and fair skin. The effect which was created when this look was juxtaposed on the brown of the Indian skin could be quite horrific.

Along with my sister Anjali and my best friend Shreeya, I went to the 'location' of the shoot, 'photo shoot' as Mr Agni liked to call it, where we were greeted by Mr Agni himself. He was a chubby, dark man with a shining head. His eyes were not to be seen behind thick, black-framed glasses. His mouth was stained a deep red from years of pan-chewing. Now that I have seen a fair share of photo studios, I can safely say that Mr Agni's place would not quite qualify as a bonafide studio. The 'studio' was more of a small, dingy room decorated with every imaginable sort of photograph pasted on the wall—photographs of smiling babies, of shy newly married couples, and of 'glam-doll' brides-to-be' (make-up courtesy Jewels). In the centre of the room were a few bright lights and black umbrellas, and a stool, sitting solitary upon a white sheet. I was slightly troubled by all of this, particularly the stool. I associated the stool with a pole, and I pictured myself propped on this wooden stool in all sorts of troubling positions.

I uneasily took my place in front of the camera and perched on the corner of the stool with a nervous smile on my face, not really knowing what to do. I was trying my best to replicate the poses that I had seen in fashion magazines and commercials, but it was really quite difficult to do this with Mr Agni behind the camera.

Just as I was starting to get used to Mr Agni's encouraging coos, the room went dark. At first, I was pretty terrified—here I was in this shady studio-of-sorts, surrounded by cameras, black umbrellas and photographs of some very strange-looking people. After a few seconds a peon came into the room and nervously explained, 'Madam . . . there is a problem with the power lines. One rickshaw driver who was slightly drunk knocked down the electricity pole.' 'Don't worry ma'am,' said Mr Agni with a bright smile, 'Only ten minutes, I just called the PWD, only five minutes, don't you worry. I will arrange for some snacks and cold drinks in the meantime.' We all knew the blackout experience—it was always something like a drunken rickshaw driver, a rainstorm, a squirrel, a bird. I really had no faith in the PWD. While ten minutes grew to thirty, which grew to sixty, and finally culminated at three hours, the three of us sat in the darkness munching on masala Uncle Chipps and sipping lukewarm Thums-Ups. I sweated like a pig under the layers of make-up and ate gingerly, trying not to disturb my lipstick.

After three hours of waiting around and hearing the

13

'Ten minutes more ma'am' line a few hundred times, a generator was finally brought in from a neighbouring store. And then there was light! I began my first ever photo shoot, hair frizzy from perspiration, my face oozing grease after the Uncle Chipps feast.

I now realize that models have it pretty tough—photo shoots are no piece of cake! As I tried to conceal my nervousness behind fake smiles and attempted to throw seductive looks at the camera, a suspicion that I was not really cut out for all this was dawning on me. Posing in front of the camera, like all other activities, does get better with experience, but one rule of thumb which became very clear to me as I later trained for the pageant was that you've got to be the proverbial peacock to shine on camera. Not just be comfortable about the way you look, but be absolutely, crazily in love with yourself. This was something that I don't think I could ever grow used to, no matter how much experience came my way.

My first photo shoot took a total of five hours and twenty-eight minutes by the clock, which is incredibly short for a full-length portfolio. At the end of it all, I was just glad to get out of that dingy studio. The gurgling of the generator, the 'Smile, Riya ma'am, smile!' from Mr Agni, and the uncomfortable feeling of trying to appear appealing and sexy in front of the camera had gotten on my nerves. I left the pseudo-studio with a promise from Mr Agni that my photos would never join the others on his wall.

What's your height?

Indians claim to have figured out the formula for success in the beauty pageant business. This claim was glorified when the country had a stretch of victories in the international arena. The formula for success, like most discoveries of substantial weight, was very simple. The success of a beauty queen, they said, depended on a few key factors—a beautiful face, a thin frame, a graceful demeanour, intelligence, and most importantly a 'good height'. All the above characteristics, expect for the last, are rampant among Indian women. The average height of an Indian woman is around five feet, which is well below the average height in the West. Thus the Miss Indian Beauties of the past were frequently among the shortest contestants at the international pageants. Based on the failure of our women in these pageants, and noticing that the winners were usually above 5' 7", the Miss Indian Beauty committee realized that this was the missing link in their current formula. They set a minimum height requirement—of 5' 6"—for entry into the pageant, and found that the taller girls were in fact more successful. Thus they formulated a simple correlation between the height of a contestant and her success rate. A 'good height' is now one of the most important factors in the making of a successful Miss Indian Beauty.

I only realized just how important the 'good height' thing was when I called the Miss Indian Beauty headquarters. I was in Mumbai for a few days, and thought it would be a good opportunity to find out more information about the contest. I got the number from the yellow pages and called. After being passed on from extension to extension, I finally got hold of Sonal, who was one of the organizers of the pageant. She sounded surprisingly young to be an organizer, and in fact I later found out that she was only twenty-three, younger than several of the girls participating in the pageant. The very first question she asked me, even before I had the chance to introduce myself was 'Darling, what's your height?'. This question was to be become the cornerstone of many conversations during my time in the pageant. I had not measured my height since I was fifteen—I approximated my height to be about 5' 9" (who cares about an inch here or there, right?). This generous figure seemed appropriate. I must have grown at least four inches since I last measured myself. I had been playing a lot of basketball, and felt sure all that stretching had helped . . . Plus, *everyone* (and I repeat, *everyone*), lies about their height in the world of Miss Indian Beauty.

That seemed to be an acceptable answer, because after a pause she said, 'Why don't you come in to meet Mr Parek today. He is my boss.' It was already 6 p.m. 'Um . . . I don't know if today is possible . . . could we do tomorrow, or the day after?' 'I really think you should come today. Mr Parek is a *very* busy man.' I hesitated. 'All right . . . in about an hour.' 'Cool, see you then!'

I figured it would be in my best interests to go and meet Mr Parek now, the man who was heading the Miss Indian Beauty committee team. This was just great—I had all of thirty minutes to get ready for my appointment! After deep (and quick) reflection I decided on an outfit, a white skirt that hit my legs at just the right spot, appropriately short, guaranteeing a second look, teamed with a pink tissue top only just flirting with sexiness. To this outfit I added my tallest pair of high heels.

Mr Parek was an unattractive man. He was in his late forties but looked well beyond his age. Short, skinny, dark and bald, he wore a strange pair of suspenders (I haven't seen anyone wear suspenders in years), and the most atrocious magenta tie. The strange suspenders and hideous ties were to become his trademark. I must say that he had very beautiful hands. They were very feminine, with long,

17

slender fingers which were always perfectly manicured and decorated with multiple rings. When I shook his hand I was surprised by its softness.

Mr Parek puzzled me, and he does till date. I am unsure of how to interpret him. He could have been one of the two—very confused, which lended him a fluffy, pseudo-philosopher appearance, or he could have been extremely cunning. His exercised fluffiness was just enough to confuse the likes of the average Miss Indian Beauty contestant.

I waited for forty-five minutes for a meeting that lasted all of five minutes. It was an ordinary meeting with pretty general questions—the expected 'What's your height?', 'What do you do?' type of thing. Though our meeting lasted just five minutes, I must have struck a pretty impressive cord with Mr Parek, and that is what would ultimately lead me to a place in the contest.

I officially entered the Miss Indian Beauty contest after sending in the signed entry form and, of course, the 'portfolio pictures' which thankfully did not turn out that badly. They were just a tad 'Indori', thanks to Jewels' glittery eyeshadow and red lipstick which looked even redder on camera. The wait began. I was back in Bhopal and had not much else to do. Because I had recently returned from a busy, hectic semester at college, I found this period to be particularly unbearable. When the clock struck nine in the morning, I would imagine myself trekking through piles of snow, Starbucks coffee in tow, late as usual for my

Economics class. Instead, here I was in Bhopal, sitting in the verandah, the sun beating down on my neck, sipping endless cups of chai. In any other situation it would have been rather enjoyable, but I felt that my life was on hold, and it was scary. I had taken quite a risk by taking a semester off from school. What if I did not even make the first cut? What would I do with my time? Would I be whiling away the next six months in Bhopal, sipping chai? The feeling of insecurity burgeoned as each day went by, making the wait unbearable.

The frustration that this situation brought with itself soon twisted into anger, when the last date of entries got pushed back fifteen days further, and then even further. I just could not understand the lack of professionalism on the part of the organizers—they had no solid dates chalked out. Pretty soon, the last date of entries had been pushed back an entire month. I called the office every day, and soon I was asking the operator about his wife and three children (Jeetu, Pinku, and Bunty aged five, four, and two respectively, if you must know).

My days revolved around waiting for that phone call. This was definitely not the life of glamour I had envisioned. The situation made me really wonder if I was the only one who cared about this contest. Wasn't anyone else interested? What were my competitors up to? Was this timeline not causing them any significant stress? Was I the only one who had a problem with the unprofessional behaviour displayed by the organizers? I felt as if my life was on hold, and there was nothing I could do about it but wait on the line for the organizers, hoping the phone would not get cut.

Finally, *finally*, lo and behold, I got the much anticipated phone call, exactly thirty-three days after I had first expected it. (And that too much beyond acceptable business hours, at 10 p.m.) I had made it through! I would have to be ready in two days to attend a pre-judging round in Mumbai. On hearing the news I rushed to tell my parents, trying to appear chilled out about the entire affair, trying very hard to suppress the excitement that I felt. It was difficult though—I was brimming over with excitement. It had finally begun—finally! My parents, too, tried to behave in the same way as I did, blasé and cool, but I saw through their facade, very much like they saw through mine. I saw my mother's eyes teary with excitement, and the strains of a smile break through my father's stern face.

The very first thing he asked me was whether I had paid a visit to the puja room to give my thanks.

Pre-judging—the beginning of it all

It is rather interesting to examine the Darwinian nature of this contest. The most beautiful individuals are sought out from a wide range of backgrounds, representing every facet of this country, covering all societies and regions. These individuals are made to compete and are then judged. It is exhilarating, intense, vicious and explosive all at the same time. When I arrived in Mumbai, I was both excited and nervous. It was very much like that tingly first-date feeling. The feeling of anticipation, shrouded by a fresh, exciting nervousness, and just a little bit of doubt. I had been dreaming about this contest for months, and now it was finally happening. Like on a first date, when you have no idea what awaits you, this too could turn out to be a life-long romance, or it could just really suck—I had absolutely no idea what to expect. The feeling that stayed with me amidst this whirlwind of activity was a sense of sheer curiosity. Who would I be competing against? Who *were* these girls?

The morning of the pre-judging is still vivid in my mind. I arrived at the Sea Queen hotel in Mumbai wearing a short purple polka dot dress which my sister in the US had shipped to me especially for this occasion, and a very uncomfortable pair of borrowed heels that were a size too big. I had not only blow-dried my hair but straightened it as well, which was really quite an effort for me. I was twenty, and I could count the number of times I had run a hairdryer through my hair. I even put on some subtle make-up, though we had been given strict instructions to arrive 'barefaced' with 'no adornments'.

I felt nervous and uneasy as I walked down the twisting marble stairs to the banquet hall, the site of the pre-judging. It really did not help that I was having considerable trouble walking in my heels. I pulled out my cellphone and desperately tried to get in touch with someone, attempting to appear busy and cool, hoping to dissipate some of the nervousness. I was taken aback at how beautiful all the girls looked. I had never seen so many good-looking girls together in one place. At first glance, they all seemed hot, fashionable and glamorous in a very flashy, showbiz kind of way. I stuck out like a sore thumb. All of a sudden I was not so confident anymore.

The number of girls overwhelmed me; pretty girls seemed to be milling around everywhere. I settled down at the back of the room, and as my habit of keen observation kicked in, I started analyzing each one of them, slowly, carefully and painstakingly. I imagined I was following the same process that I do when I edit an economics paper, and I soon started seeing flaws in many of them. They weren't really *that* hot, or for that matter, *that* fashionable. To make myself feel better, I methodically scrutinized each one of my competitors for defects—this one had not-so-toned abs, that one had fat thighs, I saw through layers of foundation to the acne below. Perhaps it was the lack of sleep the night before, or maybe it was because I was so overwhelmed by the situation at hand, but gradually, all the pretty faces started merging into one. I could not tell one hair colour apart from another, and it was getting increasingly difficult for me to critique any longer, so I made myself as comfortable as I possibly could in my squeaky chair, and continued to sit and stare into space, waiting for something to happen.

The interview was apparently a rather basic procedure, or so my fellow competitors said. The procedure would start with the 'swimsuit round', for which we would walk down the ramp clad in the one-piece swimsuits (no 'two-pieces', i.e. bikinis, were allowed) that we had brought with us. Following this, there would be the 'evening gown' round, and then a short interview with the judges. This sounded like a seemingly simple procedure, but the combination of fifty girls and fifteen somewhat inept organizers (headed by Sonal) turned it into quite a situation.

After what seemed like hours of waiting, the process finally began at 1 p.m., even though we had been told to report at 10 a.m. sharp. Before we started we were each carefully examined to make sure we had not a trace of make-up on, and that all jewellery was off. I felt as if I was back in high school and the prefect was going down the line, checking our nails to make sure they were neat and tidy, as we all anticipated embarrassment when one of us would be singled out and made to clip our nails in front of the other girls. Some girls had to be told multiple times (but there was no apparent embarrassment) before they reluctantly took off their eyeliner and mascara.

Following this examination we had our measurements taken, the most important of which was our height. Most of us were shocked (or maybe not *that* shocked), to find that we were an inch (some of us more than that) shorter than what we had thought ourselves to be. I mean really, who has *actually* ever properly measured themselves, right? We all approximate our height, and then add an inch or so to make sure we get it right. There were even a handful of girls present who did not meet the 5' 6" height cut-off. My heart went out to them. Imagine, all your hopes and dreams of becoming a beauty queen shattered, just because you always thought you were half-an-inch taller. How very unfortunate. I recall an interesting incident, which I observed from my strategically placed seat, where I was in close proximity to the measuring tape, keenly observing the ongoing process. Preeti, a contestant from Meerut, who had recently moved to Mumbai solely to pursue her Miss Indian Beauty dream measured just 5' 5½" on tape and therefore did not quite meet the height cut-off. When she heard this, she had something close to a nervous breakdown on the spot. Sensing her extreme anxiety, the humane girl in charge of the measurement noted her height as 5' 6" and waved her off with a wink. Unfortunately, this kind effort came to no avail, as Preeti never made it to the competition.

I walked down the ramp for the very first time that day. I had no idea what to do, and tried to impersonate the graceful sway of arms and hips that I had seen on FTV, the channel I had been religiously watching for over an hour a day to prepare myself for the pageant. I wobbled down the ramp in my heels, wearing a one-piece swimsuit which was a little too small for me, put on a pained smile, and tried to look the judges straight in the eye, as we had been strongly advised to do. I hated it from the moment I stepped on to the ramp. Maybe it was due to the fact that I had not worn a pair of heels in the past three months, or maybe it was because I was trained by my Independence Day parade marching from my schooldays to walk in that extremely militaristic fashion, but I never, despite endless hours of

25

practice for those twenty-five days, got the hang of the catwalk.

By the time the swimsuit round was over, despite my rather unpleasant experience on the ramp, some of my feelings of nervousness finally began to melt away. At first glance many of the girls appeared beautiful, but after my keen analysis the defects were pretty obvious. It was around this time that I became aware of the 'Indira, Indira Chaterjee, the *SUPER*model' whispers that were going around the room. Who was this girl, everyone wanted to know. No one around me really looked like a supermodel, or at least what I imagined a supermodel might look like. I had not heard of Indira Chaterjee either, though the name sounded vaguely familiar. A tall, skinny girl sporting a pixie haircut and a severe case of acne commented, '*Yaa* . . . , I thought she was on the jury, but *arre* she is a contestant, now we are all dead. *Finished!*' My curiosity grew, and so I asked around and sniffed out our 'supermodel' contender. Indira was a pretty girl, but it was in a plain Bengali way, with the clear fair skin endowed by God to Bengali women. With large, close-set almond-shaped eyes, she was not too tall, nor did she have the skinny, chic body that I expected from a supermodel. I was neither overly impressed nor too intimidated by Indira Chaterjee. I did not understand what the hype was all about.

By this point in time I was too exhausted to continue my acute analysis, which was getting to be rather tiring anyway, so I changed into a plain black cocktail dress which I wore in lieu of an 'evening gown', as I did not own one, and once again retired to my seat.

It was during the time when we all sat waiting in our eclectic assortment of evening gowns, in alphabetical order, that I first met Miriam, who would be my roommate and saviour during the murderous twenty-five days of training. Over the past few hours I had developed a mental routine that I went through for every girl I laid eyes on. I would systematically analyze her looks and body, her dress sense, and her chances of winning the crown. This was not exactly the healthiest way to begin a relationship, but hey, it was a beauty pageant after all.

Miriam struck me as a very laid-back and relaxed person, and this observation was confirmed over the course of the month. Miriam had moved to Muscat at a very young age and been to Spain and the USA for college, where she had studied aerospace engineering, but had dropped out due to a shortage of funds. After graduating she had joined Emirates airlines to work as a stewardess. (Of all things, after nearly obtaining a degree in aerospace engineering!) Over the course of the pageant, Miriam kept much to herself and spent her time either talking to me, or on her cellphone. She was not loud and obstructive like some of the others, but instead, kept a low profile, which was definitely the smarter way to go. Most people thought Miriam was South Indian due to her dark complexion and sharp features. Miriam may not have been a classic beauty of any sorts, but her face had a certain charm, in that very sharp, chic, model kind of way. I could see her making it big as a ramp model, if only she could lose her belly. Standing tall at 5' 9", she had a willowy frame, but two years of being a stewardess (which I swear is such an unhealthy career) had given her a belly. This was the result of the massive water retention that the body undergoes when one spends so much time in the air. She had an OK sense of style. In fact, she did not really have a well-defined personal style, but she was well-dressed and wore semi-trendy clothing. Did she have a good chance at winning the crown? Perhaps. She would definitely make it to the top ten, I thought. She was tall, and she had a personality. I didn't really see her as a Miss Indian Beauty—if she won she would definitely be the dark horse.

Miriam and I 'clicked' right away. After the last four hours of mental analysis, now that I was running low on cellphone credit, it was nice to be able to critique (or more aptly put, gossip) with someone who was on the same wavelength. I remember the good time we had examining the peculiar evening gowns that some of the girls donned. The gowns came in all shapes and sizes. Some wore long, sequinned gowns, while others wore tiny 'cocktail dresses' that landed right below (or on) the hips, revealing dark-brown butt cheeks. This was really not what I had imagined when I thought of an evening gown. Some wore turtleneck dresses while others had dresses with some rather breathtaking décolleté. Some wore dresses in unimaginable shades of neon, whereas others displayed polka dots and stripes. All in all, it was a fun exercise for the both of us to rate each one of the 'exquisite' gowns.

The evening gown round was even more uncomfortable than the swimsuit round, though this time we were fully clothed. We not only had to walk down that godforsaken ramp, but actually go stand in front of the judges in batches of ten and get examined from all sides and angles. I felt like I was a caged animal in a zoo. I almost expected our two esteemed judges, Mr Parek and Miss Rani Savan, the editor of a leading Indian fashion magazine, to come up to each one of us and ask us to lift up our dresses!

The next step was the very first in the slow elimination process that was to follow through the course of the next twenty-five days. Sonal came and announced that the judges would like to meet some of us individually. She claimed that this was in no way a reflection of who was to be selected (yeah, right), but the judges wanted to see how some of us 'projected our voice'. As the list progressed down the rank of numbers, I would see the crestfallen faces of the girls who were not called for an 'interview'. When my number came around and I was told to meet the judges, I was rather relieved. As expected, they asked me the infamous 'what's your height' question (though they had my newly measured height in front of them on paper), and then Rani, after taking a long look at my professional resume, asked me why, after doing all the things that I had done, including so much social work, did I want to run for the Miss Indian Beauty pageant. I replied that if I became a Miss Indian Beauty, I would leverage my fame to help those who could not help themselves. I realized through the conversation that this was the way I had justified the pageant to myself. If I did indeed win, I couldn't imagine myself as a professional model or a Bollywood actress, but I wanted the fame that a title brought, to be able to do all the things that I had wanted to.

The minute I was done with my thirty-second interview, I used the excuse of a departing flight and got out of there as fast as I possibly could. At that point I really did not care to wait and see who made the cut and who did not—I just wanted to flee the site, and I did just that without looking back even once.

We were to be informed of the honourable judges' decision in a week, and so once again I waited for what was to be a very long week to pass by. I busied myself with my forthcoming interview at an investment bank for a summer position. I, being my Wellesley self, needed to hedge this risk that I was taking with my life. If I secured a summer position, I would have a place to go to, something to look forward to, even if I did not make it in the pageant. I had some rather lofty aspirations—maybe I could be an investment banker *and* a beauty queen. I could bring a whole new twist to the image of a beauty queen. I could imagine myself in a smart black suit, pearls, cufflinks and the silk Miss Indian Beauty sash around my shoulder. No skimpy bikinis for me. Now that would *really* set me apart. I then tried to block out all thoughts of the pageant and distracted myself with the world of bulls and bears.

I finally got the congratulatory call seven days later at 9 p.m., and I was more relieved than excited, because I had withdrawn from the semester at Wellesley that very day. Perhaps the most challenging twenty-five days of my life were about to begin . . . and I had all of five days to prepare for them.

Little did I know what went behind the preparation for a beauty pageant. Mental preparation, getting into shape, the so-called 'grooming classes'—all of that began several months in advance, but I was now confronted with the task of preparing and packing my 'trousseau' for the month. So, what does one pack for a beauty pageant? I refused to do any sort of elaborate packing or preparation for this pageant. I was an idealist, America had made me that. I had decided that I would just be myself. I was not going to pretend to be some hot-shot model or fashionista, because I was not, and if I tried to be I would probably make a fool of myself. I was pretty close to it already by merely deciding to take part. I was going to be true to myself as well as to everyone else, and just *be* who I was. In the world of beauty pageants that proved to be easier said than done.

To begin my packing I first threw into my suitcase an assortment of clothes from my wardrobe, pretty much the basic clothing that any normal college-going twenty-year-old would have—several pairs of flip-flops (which I unfortunately never got the chance to wear), a few pairs of high heels (which were in pieces by the end of the show), a few make-up items, and at the last minute I hesitantly added a blow-dryer and hair-straightener. We had been told to bring a sari or two, and a few dresses for the 'formal functions' that we would be attending, so I had my mom's tailor fit me for a few plain blouses.

It was only later on through the course of the twenty-five days that I was to become aware of the extent of preparation that went into this pageant. Girls began their 'grooming classes', which included classes with a bunch of phony Page 3-ers, who taught you how to hold your fork and knife, how to sit like a lady, how to lay down like a lady, and other such nonsense, all the things that those who could afford to pay the outrageous prices for the classes probably already knew.

Several girls (like myself) went on hardcore diets and weight-loss programs to get in shape for the upcoming pageant. In addition to all of this, a few girls had spent close to Rs 5 lakh on purchasing outfits, shoes and bags for this pageant. Many came with packets of clothes, shoes, and bags specifically tagged for each one of the twenty-five days. Several girls complained of clearing out their bank accounts, and borrowing money from their parents to shop and 'prepare' for the pageant.

Another trend which I was not aware of was that designers sponsor wardrobes for the girls for the course of the training period, in the hope that their designs would get some publicity through the extensive coverage that the pageant received.

In an extreme case, one of the contestants, Stephanie, applied the year before and got through the preliminary round, but decided not to participate in the pageant as she wanted to earn more money through modelling to 'prepare' a wardrobe for the pageant. Gathering her trousseau for the pageant had been her occupation for the last year. Personally I felt that this so-called 'prep' was in vain. I doubt that it made any difference to who finally won or lost, but it made some girls feel more self-assured as to the way they looked, and perhaps instilled a sense of security.

It was all happening now. I stood with my suitcase by the car, ready to bid my parents adieu. 'OK guys, I guess this is goodbye . . .' Why the hell were my parents getting teary-eyed now? I mean, I was away in the US most of the year anyway. The training program was for only one month, and that too in Mumbai, just a short flight away. 'Beta . . . we will come to visit you next weekend, OK? We will stay at your hotel only.'

'No, Mom! Don't be crazy . . . there is no need for that. Please now . . . stay calm.' Oh God, were those *tears* in my *dad's* eyes? All this emotion was getting a tad infectious, and I felt my chin quivering. Please, I told myself, *please* don't cry. For some reason this felt like a big step in my life. I guess it was. This was a childhood fantasy that I had finally mustered up the guts to try and make real. It was probably the same for my parents. This was so different from anything that anyone in my family had ever done. In my family, not getting a PhD was going against tradition! My mother broke my stream of thought. 'Beta . . . remember to eat well. Who knows what they will give you to eat. Do you want me to pack some namkeen—the non-fried kind?'

'No mom that won't be necessary.' I might never make it to Mumbai at this rate, I thought. We said our final goodbyes and I got into the car. I felt a piece of rice on my nose. Must have come from the tilak that my mom had pasted on my forehead. I wiped it off. I wish they had not made such a big deal about this. It had made me nervous. I wanted to think of this as a random vacation or summer camp, but now, after all that drama, it was feeling like a lot more than that.

34

On your marks, get set, *go!*

2 April—the day when it all finally began. The Miss Indian Beauty contest, the place where dreams are built and shattered. I entered the plush marble lobby of the Grand Hotel, our very own personal Tihar jail for the next twenty-five days. On checking in, I was elated to find that Miriam was to be my roommate for the month. Within just a few minutes of checking in, we were whisked away to CG's, the banquet hall in the basement of the Grand Hotel, where most of our 'training sessions' were to take place. As we went through the month-long period, most of our time was spent at CG's, which was kept closely guarded from the eyes of the public. It was used for multiple purposes—everything from a dining hall to an exercise room to a make-up room, and even a dance studio. This was the first time I would lay my eyes on the chosen ones. I recognized most of the girls, as I had spent a fair amount of time

pondering over which ones I would have the pleasure of meeting again. There were a few faces that I did not recognize, but that was probably because several of them looked startlingly different with the layers of make-up they now had on. I felt out of place with my just-out-of-bed hair (and no, that was not done on purpose) and puffy eyes, dressed in baggy, creased white linen pants and a loose pink t-shirt, sporting my favourite pair of pink rubber flip-flops. I was quite shocked to see the twenty-two others (as only one girl had not yet showed up) sporting three-inch heels, styled hair and make-up at this hour of the morning.

As we took our seats in the circle of chairs, I realized for the first time how different each of these twenty-three girls were. The set ranged from short (all 5' 6" or taller, mind you), fair and plump, to tall, dark and lanky. Some sat quietly, unadorned and unmade, in fairly plain clothing, crouched back in their chairs, absorbing all the glitter around them, whereas others smiled and cooed through glittery mouths about high-fashion, runways and society columns. I wondered where I figured in the scene set before me. I could not place myself with the quiet, unassuming types. I had never really been part of the scenery at any point in my life, and I did not intend to be this time round either. Though I may not have been very fashionable, nor too stylish, I would have to find a way to set myself apart in this scene. I had lived in nine cities, and attended ten different schools across four continents. At each place, I had not only survived, but I had lived happily. I would have to find a niche for myself in this world too. It was an old theory of mine that people can be categorized by their shoes, so as we lounged around in CG's, making small talk with each other, I went from chair to chair, face to face, one pair of shoes to the next. Most girls had really icky shoes, I would never have dreamt of wearing any of those. One pair of feet was irritating me in particular. They belonged to Prachi. The first time I saw Prachi I had thought that she was quite pretty, with her fair skin and small features, but she had this abnormally long ostrich neck. She was one of the tallest of the group and had a slim, slender frame, but was saddled with an unfortunately lumpy body which popped out in all directions when wearing a particularly tight outfit. She was wearing this awful pair of golden-brown sandals with silver straps and block heels. The shoes looked like they were ten years old. The golden colour was flaking away, and they really needed a wash. Prachi had rather large feet and her shoes did not seem to fit her right. Her feet slipped out at least an inch into the front, and her long and unattractive toes (which were coloured in chipping nail polish of a gaudy shade) were dangling out over the top of her shoes. Were her toes touching the floor? I was feeling a bit nauseous looking at this pair of feet. It was time to move on.

My eyes landed on a really fabulous pair of baby-blue suede stilettos. Much better. Were those Jimmy Choos?

They had to be. . . . I looked up at the face that owned the fab shoes. It was Juhi. I began the analysis procedure that I had perfected during the pre-judging round. At twenty-five, Juhi was the oldest of the contestants. She was a Punjabi *kudi* from Chandigarh whose father was in the army. After she graduated from college (with great difficulty) she went on to become a stewardess for Singapore Airlines for over five years, until she was 'discovered' on a flight. For the past year she had been modelling in Delhi for some pretty impressive names. Juhi gave off the notorious image of a model who sleeps around to make money . . . and who might perhaps sleep around to win the crown. Whenever I saw Juhi, the word 'hag' came straight to mind. Being a stewardess for over five years had played a toll on her skin too, and she was in dire need of anti-ageing products. Her sleek haircut added to her bad-girl-'I-sleep-around'-model look. She had a great body, though, with perfect proportions. Maybe people are right when they say that sex is the best form of exercise. I was to discover that out of the entire group, Juhi's sense of style was the best. She had a fabulous collection of shoes, ranging from slippers to sneakers to stilettos.

Could she win? Probably not. That is, if the judges were smart enough to see through her assumed-chic look, at the tired, twenty-five-year-old with vanishing dreams of fame and stardom that she really was, for whom this was the last chance to make it big.

I was jolted back to reality as Sonal made us familiar with the rules of the pageant—no leaving the group at any point during the day, no leaving the premises of the hotel, no guests (except during visiting hours on Sunday), no food (except what we were served at CG's), no alcohol, no cigarettes, no skipping any sessions. 'You are here for a reason girls, and that reason is to be trained . . .' Wow, I thought. I had never been in such a constricted environment at any point in my life. I felt as if I was back in my Catholic all-girls' boarding school, though this time around instead of chalkboards we had a catwalk, instead of ribboned plaits we had styled, hair-sprayed puffs, and instead of knee-length, starched, pleated skirts, we had racy, revealing swimsuits. Though the Grand Hotel was a top of the line, brand new seven-star hotel, every morning I woke up thinking of the concrete walls, alarm clocks and curfews of grade school.

It was the first time that Mr Parek, the man behind the plan, would speak to us as a group. Even though I had had the good fortune of meeting him before, this was the first time that I was to hear him address us as a team. We were still a group of twenty-three; the twenty-fourth contestant, Indira Chaterjee, as I had rightly guessed, had not yet arrived. I could feel the growing sense of curiosity about her whereabouts, as well as a rising yet tactically concealed apprehension about her absence. Mr Parek, at the age of fifty-three, was the MD of Glamour Infotainment, and over the past twenty years he had risen through the ranks of the Glamour Group to hold this coveted position. (Which man would not want to be the benign hand behind the making of a beauty queen?) He was a self-proclaimed movie-buff, critic, and to my utmost irritation, philosopher. (Let me reiterate, this is all self-declared.) He had held this extremely desirable position for the past three years, and other than the Miss Indian Beauty contest, he handled a radio station called Masala FM and produced low-budget movies. He was succeeding a certain Mr Pradip Ruia, a legend in the business of producing beauty queens. It was under Mr Ruia's shrewd supervision that the first training program was launched close to a decade ago, after Mamta Sindhu, suffering a close defeat at the Miss Universal Beauty pageant, came back with advice on the creation and making of a beauty queen. She spoke of the intensive and structured programs which certain South American countries such as Venezuela and Brazil had adopted that had lead to unimaginable successes in the world of beauty pageants. It was under Mr Ruia that such programs were constructed to fit the Indian framework, and soon India became a pretty damn strong competitor in the international beauty pageant arena.

Mr P (as I fondly grew to call Mr Parek) was now

desperate. He was under immense pressure from the board. For the past three years, under his management, India had not produced a single winner on the international level. To be perfectly honest, we had not really come close to it either. The ex-Miss Indian Beauties of the past three years had been lost in the sad amnesia of the glamour business, breathing the filmy air of Lokhandwala, struggling in the sea of Bollywood, ready to do anything to reach the limelight which they had felt for a moment. Mr P wanted that international crown to his name. It was high time, said the board of directors, we need some results. Now. The fact of the matter was that it was absolutely necessary for Mr P to produce a winner this year, and we all realized this. The institution that Mr Ruia had strived to create was sinking as a whole into the quicksand of beauty pageants.

Across the globe, too, beauty pageants as an institution were losing their hold, plummeting downwards into the ocean of oblivion. In several countries, particularly in the Western world, they had lost all their gravity. They were slowly but steadily being written off as poor attempts at instant stardom. Only recently, Miss America received a jolt as they got the ditch from their long-time sponsor, as viewer ratings dived to an all time low. In the time and age of reality TV shows, as new and more interesting, novel paths to fame were being paved, the harsh truth was that beauty pageants had a stale, unpleasant air surrounding them, and people didn't want a whiff. Would Miss Indian

Beauty suffer the same end? Well, if it vanished into thin air, like several beauty pageants already had, so would Mr P.

As Mr P launched into his pseudo-intellectual speech, several girls sat upright, noting down everything he said word-by-word. I yawned, reminded of sleepy lectures at Wellesley. He spoke of the 'expert training' that we would be receiving, the morals and values that we must hold close to our hearts, how the competition should be taken in a good spirit, and so on. All the ABCs of a usual opening speech. On that day we all realized that there were twenty-four of us, but there would only be three winners, and of those three, only one would be Miss Indian Beauty. The rest of us would go home empty-handed, carrying with us only a shattered dream.

Meeting our 'trainers'

There are a few names synonymous with the Miss Indian Beauty pageant, and the two most celebrated of these were Emma Contractor, an authority on speech and diction, and Donald Singh, fitness guru for the world of Bollywood. These two names had been associated with the pageant for close to fifteen years now, and had probably achieved much of their fame thanks to the publicity they had received from the contest over the years. We would soon have the pleasure of meeting them both.

She walked in looking oh-so-chic in her tweed suit, wearing dark Chanel sunglasses, carrying her signature green Harrods bag in her manicured hands, fingernails painted blood-red. She was tiny and dainty, and her hair, a stylish bob, was dyed a deep red-brown. Though she was a full-blooded Indian, she seemed very 'angrez'. For her, this was just another year of Miss Indian Beauty. Like the past years, this year too would be the same, as would the ones to follow. For her, all of this was just so passé. Mrs Contractor had begun her career as a socialite, after which she rose to fame by hosting a popular TV show that had aired on national television in the late eighties, and then progressed to owning a few happening nightclubs in Mumbai. How she got into speech and diction training is a bit of a mystery.

Emma Contractor had been involved with the Miss Indian Beauty pageant for a long time now, and had become part and parcel of the institution. To all of us she came across as this stylish figure straight out of Page 3, who was just sort of *there*, but did not really have any concrete purpose. She was nice, sweet and mildly entertaining, and I'm sure she enjoyed all the fawning girls, but her sessions were rather useless. Her role reminded me somewhat of the Queen of England, of someone who came with a flourish, made us gasp with awe, and who was gone just as quickly. For me, Mrs Contractor's sessions were the ultimate bore as we sat and read out unending lists of words, examined homophones, antonyms, synonyms and similar things of zero consequence to a beauty queen. Her role was to get us into shape for the très important Q&A round, but her sessions really ended up being more like a bad grammar class.

Mrs Contractor's first session, like all firsts, was

exciting. Exciting in that fresh, first day of school sort of way, when you arrive with hopes of being the 'cool' one, and try to etch out a niche for yourself. It was especially important because this was the first time that we were to formally introduce ourselves to the group. This would be the very first time that we would not only be examined by Mrs Contractor, but also by each other. As each girl came in front of the group to present herself, a few girls took notes, making comments on the flaws and strengths of their competitors. I could see faces become alert as someone turned out to be particularly well-spoken, and relax when somebody fumbled or struggled to form even simple English sentences.

For the very first time, each one us got a tangible sense of the competition that was to be. This was the day that first impressions were formed, and I firmly believe that first impressions are often the last.

In view of my constant goal of weight loss I had become rather obsessed with the whole fitness thing. I had been on all sorts of diets—Atkins, South Beach, no-carb, no-fat— you name it, and I had probably experimented with it at some point. Therefore I was quite eager to meet Donald Singh. He was the man who for the past eleven years had trained the Miss Indian Beauty girls, the man who moulded your ordinary, girl-next-door into a Miss Indian Beauty and perhaps even a Miss Universal Beauty. This was the man who had the power to transform gawky teenagers into curvaceous beauty queens, the man who had shaped so many voluptuous bodies. By what means, physical, mental or surgical, is questionable.

He walked in, a stocky, short man dressed in striped pants and orange shoes, clothes that perfectly suited his cartoon-character name. A name which quite cleverly disguised the strict, militaristic, physical trainer that he really was. He had a twinkle in his eye and a bounce in his step (which probably came from training some very good-looking girls over the course of eleven years), and was to become the scourge in our lives for the next one month. He was the man who would tear us out of our warm beds at five o'clock in the morning, and the face we would think of while drinking juices of the most disquieting colours.

All throughout Emma's class he had sat at the back of the room and carefully observed each one of us. The second she left, he marched up to the front of the room and immediately launched into details of the month to be. So this was the deal. Waking up and working out at five-thirty in the morning was probably the better part of the deal. The 'satwik' diet that we each had to follow was far worse, and became the bane of our existence for the duration of that month.

Next we met Yasmeen Wadia, model-turned-fashion

designer-turned-interior decorator-turned-choreographer. Yasmeen did not really look like the model type. She was not really that tall or thin, and though she was pretty, it was in a very ordinary way. She had that ubiquitous pretty Indian face that was on every street corner. Back in her prime, which was only about five years ago, she had haunted some of the top Indian runways, but when her career came to an end fairly quickly, her adept social skills led her to new professions.

Over the course of those twenty-five days we were to spend a big chunk of our time with Yasmeen, more so than with any of our other trainers. The very special thing about Yasmeen that really struck me was the fact that she could change roles with the snap of a finger. From the inspiring mother-figure to the evil, brutal teacher, from the compassionate sister to the understanding friend, she was truly an all-purpose, all-in-one-package, edging close to schizophrenia, but not quite there yet. As the days went by, I discovered that Yasmeen played several roles, some of which I never did fully understand. Her roles ranged from teaching ungainly girls like me to do the catwalk to conducting Emma-like Q&A sessions, from putting together our outfits for the various events that took place to choreographing the finale.

To me, Yasmeen was more of a friend than anything else, and perhaps that's the reason why I never could learn that catwalk. (I swear, only a Nazi could teach that to me.)

She was that someone who I could always confide in, that someone who I could go and bitch to, that someone I would go to when the pressure got a bit too much. But at times I wondered how much I could really tell her, to what degree I could really trust her, and to what extent her opinion really mattered. I wondered to what extent all of this, much like everything else, was just a facade.

I still remember that uncomfortable moment when Yasmeen went down the line, asking each one of us about our modelling experience. We were really quite an eclectic bunch. We had girls present who had modelled for the top tier of Indian designers, yet were a long way from being proclaimed supermodels. There were a few girls who had not had a lot of runway experience, but had done a lot of print and commercial work, and then there was me, with zero experience. The majority of the group had had some experience, be it at college fashion shows, or even China Fashion Week, but I had nil. This was where I was lagging behind most, and was the strongest drawback that would end up pulling me down.

After having been through endless formalities on day one— the introductions, the inspiring speech, the passing around of textbooks (in our case a book of quotes and beauty pageant questions), we retired to our rooms for the night.

As we all got to know our partners for the month, Miriam and I sat down to have a full discussion on each contestant. This was to be the very first in a long series of discussions on this topic, until it really got to be quite mundane and we realized the futility of it. We lay down on our luxurious beds, under the starched white linen sheets, our heads resting on down pillows, and talked through the night (even though we had to be up before sunrise for the workout), analyzing in great detail each and every candidate. From her hair to her speech, from her lipstick to her shoes, we covered it all. It was only the next day that we realized that this very discussion had taken place in every single room.

That night, as our eyes strained to shut, but the energy that newness brings kept us awake, I felt much like I did on my first day of school, not knowing what to expect, not knowing what would happen, or who my friends would be. I lay awake in anticipation of what the coming month would hold. The thoughts of nervousness and competition had been temporarily overshadowed by the shine of novelty that this experience brought. I felt as if I had reverted back to my days at boarding school, where we had teachers to answer to, curfews to meet, and strict rules to follow. As I finally gave in to the fatigue of the day and shut my eyes, my mind was clouded with thoughts. I could see the eager faces of the girls, I could see our trainers, I saw Emma's blood-red nails, Donald's striped pants and glowing forehead (I always wondered if that glow arose from his holistic lifestyle or premature balding), my family, and the puppy-dog smile on Rushab's face. But behind it all, glittering in the backdrop, I could see the crown clearly, magnificent in its grandeur, dazzling and sparkling with diamonds and gems, and I think every single one of us dreamt of it on that first night.

Cleansing the mind, body and soul

Mind over matter, mind over body, mind over all. This was what the satwik was hoping to achieve. Yes, I know, it doesn't really make too much sense, and nor did the diet to me. I must say, before I begin to bash the diet, that despite the bouts of diarrhoea and constipation that we all went through, despite the breakouts that we all suffered (we all swore it was the overdose of nuts), despite the food-obsessed, starved individuals that we all grew to become, the diet did make us all feel healthier and supplied us with the energy that we would need to get through the gruelling days ahead. Oh yeah, some of us did lose weight, but I, despite the diet, ironically gained 0.9 kg.

Our diet was meat-free, wheat-free, milk-free, and starch-free. That meant no chicken, no milk (no more chai for me), no rotis, white rice or potatoes. We started off our day with two glasses of vegetable juice: carrot, tomato, bitter gourd, spinach and sometimes papaya. For breakfast we were served fruits and nuts. For our midday snack, three hours after breakfast, we were served raw sprouts (according to Donald, this was the only source of live energy) with rock salt, chopped tomatoes and onions (let me tell you, there was a run for those onions every day), and vinegar dressing. For lunch we had dal (methi or palak), one vegetable of the likes of tori, spinach or another one from that healthy family (cooked in one teaspoon of olive oil), with either wild rice or non-wheat rotis made from bajra, methi or jawar. For our evening snack we were served more juices of varying colours and textures, along with more nuts and dry fruits. For dinner we had the same as we did for lunch, except that there would be an extra vegetable dish. On rare occasions we would be given wholewheat pasta, and this was always a source of huge excitement for the force. Fruit accompanied every meal. We were allowed to consume as much as we wanted at every meal, though some of the chubbier girls were made to stop eating rice, rotis and dry fruit.

So this was what aspiring beauty queens were fed. There we were, Miss Indian Beauty hopefuls emulating the austere existence of the sages of eons gone by, to discover our pure, chaste, primitive selves with the help of the purifying, refining and rejuvenating satwik diet.

5.30 a.m. 'Good morning ma'am, this is your first wake-up call!'

5.45 a.m. 'Good morning ma'am, this is your second wake-up call!'

Neither of these calls managed to wake us up that morning, though just ten minutes later I kicked myself hard and wished I had indeed heeded those calls. As we lay there in our deep slumber, the incessant bell-ringing and knocking started. Very soon, the knocking turned to thumping, and the ringing grew even more persistent. Miriam dragged herself out of her warm, comfortable bed, but I refused to budge. A waiter came in with four glasses of a vile-looking green liquid which he insisted was juice, and along with him came an entire camera crew—two cameramen, three reporters, and a few people with mikes. I was too groggy to react to all of this, and for a minute I thought I was dreaming and buried myself deep under the safety of the covers. It was only minutes later that I realized where I was, and what was going on. I had left the safe haven of my home in good old Bhopal, and was now defenceless in alien territory. There was a camera crew in my bedroom at 5.45 a.m. Was this even legal? As I lay there buried under the covers I tried to think of an escape plan. The cameras couldn't see me like this! I was wearing my blue cotton PJs with the growing hole in the backside, the pyjama set that I prided myself on owning since the age of ten. I desperately racked my mind for an escape plan as I saw the glaring lights of the camera slowly penetrating the cotton covers. I mustered up all the courage that I possibly could at that ungodly hour, flung off the covers, threw a sheet on to the camera (which due to a lack of coordination, I missed), and rushed into the bathroom, my only asylum. I then busied myself attempting to look presentable. I washed the morning shine off my face, brushed the stale breath away, and put in my contact lenses so I could at least see what was happening. I had firmly made up my mind to stay in the refuge of my bathroom until these camera people had left, but I soon decided otherwise as the thumping began on the bathroom door. I knew these people wouldn't go away till I emerged and gave them a statement, so I stepped out of the bathroom and into the harsh focus of the camera as elegantly as I possibly could, desperately trying to conceal that hole in my pyjama-bottoms. It is still not clear to me what I actually said to the camera people that morning, but all I know is that it was aired on public television, and the entire world saw that hole in my PJs. How I wish I had woken up to those wake-up calls.

After having answered some extremely irritating questions, I gulped down the glasses of so-called juice (I think this was the only time that I drank it), pulled on my sports bra, tracks and sneakers, and ran down to the terrace garden where our workout was to be held, desperately trying to straighten out my hair in the elevator. I had a strong feeling that there would be cameras present at our morning workout too.

I honestly do not think I have ever been awake so bright and early. Even though I had never woken up at this hour, I certainly had stayed up this late (or this early?), the reason at times being a fabulous party, but on most occasions I was burning the midnight oil at the library during exam time. As I walked up to the terrace garden (where we would be working out), I was quite surprised to see how decked up some of the girls were simply to exercise, and that too this early in the morning! How the hell did they motivate themselves to put on lipliner and mascara at 5.30 a.m.? Many of the girls wore outfits with matching socks and headbands, and a few of them even sported matching sneakers. The most peculiar thing though was that many of the girls had left their hair down. This seemed particularly strange to me as I have fairly long hair, and cannot even fathom the idea of working out with my hair hanging down loose. Here were girls with hair far longer than mine (in some cases it even hung below their waists), lying loose while they exercised.

Over the course of that one month I saw girls sport some rather bewildering clothing, but it was always these morning workout outfits that amused me the most. Girls would go to great lengths to match bras (and no, they were not sports bras) to their socks. From peach satin capris (with fake Nike signs to justify the usage for sports) to tennis skirts (to do yoga!), to plaid boxer shorts to leather dungarees, I saw it all in that one month.

I had always considered myself to be quite a workout buff. I had been an athlete in school and a gym rat ever since I could remember, and therefore I was curious about the hype that surrounded Donald Singh's workouts. I had not expected any of this holistic health prattle. When he told us his workout was 'unconventional' but very strenuous, I figured he meant tai-chi, pilates or something along those lines, but what we got was something absolutely unanticipated.

We always started off our workout with yoga-ish breathing exercises, and it was at this time that Donald would start off with his wistful mumbo-jumbo, the whole 'mind over matter, mind over body' and 'I am part of the universe and the universe lies within me' kind of stuff. I have to admit that on that first day, as we lay down in the damp grass and felt the dew seeping up our bottoms (thankfully we got mats later), it was refreshing to stare up into the newness of the morning and take in the vastness and splendour of the morning sky. The workout was the one and only time that we were let out of our cages into the great outdoors and given the chance to take in some fresh air (though I wonder how 'fresh' one could call the air in Mumbai), and sometimes I would savour these mornings for what they were, a time for the caged animals in us to run free.

56

Our workout comprised of a series of exercises which were a mixture of stretching, military boot camp, and some rather innovative calisthenics. We would do things like bunny-hops, frog jumps, push-ups, running around in circles while flapping our arms, squats, lunges, etc. It was never organized or planned, and I seriously questioned the effectiveness of the workout. After Donald finished up with his bit, we were put into groups where his team of trainers would instruct us on abs, thighs and hips, the communal problem areas. For most of us the workout was a real drag, and of no real consequence. We all went through the exercises as one would a mandatory dental checkup, with indifference and lethargy. It was only during that last portion of the workout, when 'abs' were mentioned, did I see faces light up with energy and eagerness. I don't know what it is about Indian women, maybe it is their genes—nearly everyone present here was thin, of a slender build, with willowy arms and legs—but for most us, our abs were the problem area, and we knew it. I have come to believe, more than ever before after this pageant, that love handles are inherent in the body of an Indian woman. I do admit that love handles look rather graceful when one wears a sari. A woman in a sari without love handles is like an Indian woman without a bindi. This inherent quality did wonders for our grandmothers and great-grandmothers, but I like wearing jeans, and love handles in jeans are absolutely no good.

After we all desperately worked away at our abs, doing countless stomach crunches and sit-ups, Donald singled out a few of the heavier girls and those who had problematic skin, and told them to stop their consumption of dal, roti and rice. They were to stick to an absolutely raw diet for the next one month, and a group of 'no rice-roti' girls was born. They were not allowed to eat anything but salad and fruit, and we would see them stare longingly at the dal, rice and rotis served to us. Even though I had not been told to stop eating dal and roti, after a week of eating the same old stuff (it all tasted surprisingly similar), I too began to follow the raw food regimen, out of utter exasperation and boredom more than anything else. To my amazement I gained nearly a kilogram in a week. Perhaps it was the nuts that I consumed, disregarding the high calories that they contained, or the excessive amounts of fruit that I was eating—I am not sure, but I never did figure out the satwik diet.

As several early mornings passed by, I developed a strong opinion on the merits and demerits of Donald's workout. I realized how much he could have done in that short one-month period if he had really wanted to make a difference. After having tried numerous diets and workouts myself, I have come to understand the female body to a certain extent, and therefore felt I could take the liberty to critique Donald's workout.

The truth of the matter is that when you have twenty-three girls, all fairly thin, ranging from the heights of 5' 6" to 5' 11", and only two hours, with limited gym space and equipment, you have a problem. There is no way that one standard workout will benefit the entire group. Perhaps the workout would suit two or three girls of a similar build and structure, but what about the remaining twenty? Also, in a situation like this, weight plays no role whatsoever. If a girl who measures 5' 11" weighs the same as a girl who is 5' 6", there could be a variety of problems. The taller girl could be underweight, or perhaps the shorter girl could be overweight, or maybe the shorter girl has a much higher percentage of muscle-mass. Therefore it was absolutely essential, if any difference was to be made over that month, for us to have each had a personalized routine. This was not impossible, as Donald brought along four assistants every day. The Grand Hotel had a small but world-class gym and whatever Donald's shortcomings, there was no doubt that he had an excellent understanding of the female body. If we had each had a meticulously planned workout, personalized for our individual body types, not only would the girls have been more encouraged to work out, but we would also have seen significantly better results.

The workouts got more and more lax as they progressed. For the first week, when the camera crew was filming our workouts, Donald Singh went all out. He would come up to our rooms to make sure we were up, and even went to the extent of making sure that we drank our juice in front of his eyes. (Of course he always brought along a cameraman.) But after the first ten days, when the cameras left, so did Mr Singh. Of course we would still see him around when he would deliver one of his holier-than-thou speeches, but after those initial ten days, we rarely caught a glimpse of him, except sometimes on television.

The Miss Indian Beauty walk

During our catwalk practice sessions, I always dreaded my turn on the ramp. Ever since I could remember, I had dreamt of walking down the ramp, elegant, graceful and oh-so-chic. When we were children, my sisters and I would take down the heaviest books off the bookshelf and balance them on our heads as we walked, in an attempt to perfect the catwalk. But now that I was actually here and doing it, it just wasn't that cool. As my turn on the ramp came about I would unsteadily take my position at the end of the ramp, uncomfortable in my new pair of heels, and walk down trying to replicate what I had seen on television and practiced in my head a million times. I was afraid that I probably appeared to be what I actually was—a wannabe who had no clue what she was doing, trying way too hard. As I tried to break out into the hip-swinging, head-turning walks of FTV, I realized for the first time how uneasy I felt on the ramp. Despite hours of practice, uncountable blisters and swollen feet, I would never grow to be relaxed and comfortable doing the catwalk. You see, modelling is much like a sport; you can learn how to play tennis or to cycle or row a boat in two days, but to become adept at it takes time and practice. Even though I walked till I could walk no more, till I flattened out the heels of all of my shoes, till my toes bled and I developed hideous blisters, I just did not get it. I slowly came to realize that maybe, just maybe, I did not have it in me to be on that ramp, to doll up, to show myself off and to do the catwalk.

I particularly remember a conversation I had with Neelam, the bimbette of the group. Neelam was a bouncy, bubbly, 'commercial' girl. To put it very simply, the Indian version of a blonde. She was the shortest of the group (at 5' 5") and did not meet the Miss Indian Beauty height cut-off of 5' 6". She claimed that Mr P had liked her face so much that he had cast her in the final twenty-four despite her height. She always wore a pair of grey contact lenses that made her big, round eyes look even bigger and rounder. Her dress-sense was nothing extraordinary, but she made an effort, and at times donned some rather fashionable outfits. She was one of the girls who had prepared her wardrobe for this contest months in advance. I don't think she had any chance of winning the crown. She was too short, and really did not have much of a personality. She said to me, 'Riya yaar, we are so *different*. I love to doll up, be on the catwalk, the whole world watching me. I love posing in front of the camera even more! This is what I want to do for the rest of my life, whereas you, *naa* . . . God only knows why you are here!'

As the days passed by, some of the other girls would ask me if I hated modelling and models. No, I would reply, certainly not, it's just that I did not have the capacity, the capability, and most importantly the inclination, to model myself to the optimum. They would then giggle back at me and bashfully tell me, 'Riya yaar, you are just too intelligent to be a model.' You would have thought that this might have made me feel better, but in fact it just made things worse. If I was so 'intelligent', then I *should* have been able to learn the bloody catwalk, I *should* have been able to pick up all this model-shodel business. After all it was just a beauty pageant—how hard could it possibly be?

Even though several girls among our group were trained models, the Miss Indian Beauty walk was new to all of us. You see, the Miss Indian Beauty walk is unique. When you walk down the ramp as a Miss Indian Beauty, you are not showing off a collection of clothes or jewellery, but rather you are showing yourself. It's like a different style of dancing, or an alternative swimming stroke—if you already know the sport, it is much easier to pick up, but at the same time one has to learn to not only perform but also grow comfortable and graceful with the new style. A walk has so many hidden facets, it is much like a classical dance form like Bharatanatyam or ballet, where every step you take, every movement you make, and every turn you take has deep meaning and significance. It is essential to build a persona around this walk, and most importantly, radiate energy and poise through every movement. Be it the twirling of a finger or the pout of a lip, every twist and turn must be performed with the utmost grace and feminity. The most distinctive feature of the Miss Indian Beauty walk, and perhaps the most difficult for me to learn, was the Miss Indian Beauty smile. That smile which must remain plastered on to your face—yet at the same time appear natural—exuding confidence and charm. So here I was trying to synchronize my hip movements with my lanky (and rather ungraceful) arms and legs, balance myself on three-inch heels, appear charming and graceful, emanate energy, and to top it all off, keep that smile plastered on through the entire process. It was definitely not as simple as I had imagined it to be.

Yasmeen would always tell us how important the catwalk was, and it was only later that I realized the importance of her advice. That one walk is essential. You only get one walk, one walk down that ramp to show the judges who you are and what you are. One walk to show for the hours of practice, one walk to wow them all, one walk to razzle, dazzle and shine.

Of all our various sessions, I dreaded Yasmeen's sessions the most. I hated walking the ramp in front of all the girls, and having everyone smirk at my attempts to appear lithe and nimble, when I felt and probably looked like an ungainly, lumbering giant thudding my way down the creaky wooden ramp. I was not the only one who had trouble with the Miss Indian Beauty walk; some of the girls who faced considerable trouble too were the ones who had lots of modelling experience, and had developed very distinct, 'modelesque' styles of walking. Stephanie, who had been modelling since the age of fifteen, had even more trouble with the walk than I did. The FTV walk that you see on haute-couture runways was a great way of showing off clothes, shoes and jewellery, but it was a trained, mechanical style, too sexual, and did not project persona or charm. These girls had to work the hardest to break out of their acquired walk and get into the refined, elegant gait of a Miss Indian Beauty.

It was quite a mission for Yasmeen to teach twenty-three girls how to walk. We had a wide range of problems—from hunched shoulders, to stiff necks, to bent knees, to loose arms, you name it and we had it. Over the course of twenty-five days many of us broke out of our former styles to adopt the Miss Indian Beauty walk, but in situations of nervousness, anxiety and high pressure (which is basically what happens during fashion shows), the deeply rooted problems would often reappear. Throughout this entire period I never really learnt how to walk a straight line in heels, much less exude confidence, poise and grace while doing the very special Miss Indian Beauty walk.

Unrest

From day one we had cameras on our back, and for someone like me, who felt uncomfortable just at the sight of a flash, this was quite disturbing. As rumours spread of hidden cameras in the bedrooms, I started spending a lot of time in the bathroom, changing there, talking on the phone there, and even enjoying illegal bars of chocolate and McDonalds burgers there. From the morning that they burst into my room, to the filming of my uneasy walk down the ramp, to filming us running to the bathroom when the bouts of diarrhoea hit (I swear it was those nuts), they were constantly buzzing around us like flies on a mission. I finally flipped when I found out that the camera people *did* in fact have a mission, and that mission was to create a reality TV show involving us! This was a bit too much. I decided to see the contract which we were made to sign at the pre-judging, to see if I was obliged to be a party to this tamasha. The other participants were enjoying the endless publicity that this pageant was receiving. It was their lifelong dream to be a part of Page 3, and now it was coming true. A reality TV show was the icing on the cupcake. Aashima was perhaps the most media-hungry of all the contestants, and because of her enthusiasm would become a favourite of the Style TV people. Being one of the oldest of the lot at twenty-four, Aashima was desperate to win the crown. She dreamed of entering Bollywood, and this pageant was to be her key to entry. Originally from Delhi, but now based in Bangkok, Aashima always boasted of being of 'royal descent'. Whatever that meant. She had one of the prettiest faces of the group—it was beautiful in a very traditional Indian way, with almond-shaped eyes, a Roman nose, and creamy skin. Her hips were her Achilles heel, though. Measuring close to forty inches, her hips were the primary cause of her distress and insecurity.

Her dress sense was nothing spectacular, and most of her wardrobe looked like it had been hurriedly picked up off the streets of Bangkok. (The streets of Bangkok can be a good source of clothing, but only if one is very selective.) She was also one of the girls who would go all-out with the make-up. She was a favourite with the camera crew and decked out every day with petal-pink blush, indigo eyeliner and ultra-glossy lips.

Did she have any chance of winning the crown? Some

girls thought so, and if she were to win, I would not have been altogether shocked.

I was the very opposite of Aashima, and for me it was a different story altogether. I was shy of home videos and passport photographs, and now I was going to be part of—of all things—a reality TV show which was going to be aired nationwide on prime time. I wondered what my high school teachers would think of me. What had happened to the perfect head girl? It just did not sink in that I was indeed a Miss Indian Beauty girl.

My relationship with the Style TV crew went through an entire cycle that ran the course of those twenty-five days. In the beginning I would snap and bite at their every command. I refused to be a part of anything that they were creating. This was all too good for the other girls, who would scrummage and fight for every second of airtime. Gradually, I softened up a bit, and began uncomfortably but politely to acknowledge their presence. I did a few of the necessary interviews. Slowly, we progressed to a first-name basis, and I even volunteered to be a part of their filming. Soon I found myself engaging in friendly chatter with the Style TV crew, and would enthusiastically give them ideas for the show. When the Style TV people finally did leave, we parted with tears. (OK, that is a bit of an exaggeration, but yes, I did lament their departure.) I grew especially close to Priya, who was the assistant producer for the show. She was a twenty-three-year-old journalist who, much like myself, considered herself to be something of an intellectual snob, and our common hatred of high-heeled shoes drew us together. It was she who would tell me to try and go with the flow of things, to look at things in a positive light, to accept the fact that I was indeed running for a beauty pageant. She told me that this was the world of the media, a world where reality did not exist. Everything was done with the purpose of disguising reality, playing make-believe was itself reality, and being myself was the biggest mistake that I could possibly make. When I later replayed the twenty-five days over and over in my head, reliving every moment, dissecting the mistakes and many faux-pas that I made, I realized that her advice had been of great consequence, and wished that I had indeed followed some of it.

Now that we were settled in our home for the month and had managed to find some sort of a foothold in this whirlwind of activity, all eyes became focussed on the glittering crown. Every conversation, at all points of the day, would always come back to the ultimate question: who had the highest chances of winning? This eventually led to the question that was burning at the back of all our minds. Where was Indira Chaterjee? Indira, the so-called supermodel, was the only contestant who had not yet arrived. She was by far the most experienced and accomplished model in the group, and this was growing to be a looming concern for all of us.

We were well into the training program now. All of us had pretty much come to terms with the 5.30 a.m. wake-up calls, the satwik diet, and even the omnipresent camera crew. When the trainers questioned the whereabouts of Indira Chaterjee, the organizers were quick to reply that she was unwell, and would be joining us shortly. For the first few days no one really delved further into the matter, as we were deeply engrossed in our activities. But as the week came to a close, we all began to wonder about Indira's whereabouts. At this point it was inevitable (after all, we were twenty-three women living together) that the gossip would begin. Rumours spread like wildfire, from room to room, across the length and breadth of the tenth floor (which was dedicated to the Miss Indian Beauty contestants), that this contest was fixed. The buzz was that Indira had received a letter of invitation from the organizers asking her to run for the pageant, and assured entry into the final twenty-four. This was a bit difficult to believe, but under those circumstances, surrounded by oestrogen and deprived of sleep, all the logic that had been drilled into my mind thanks to years of education seemed to dissipate, and I too wholeheartedly indulged in the juicy gossip.

All the dirty Miss Indian Beauty gossip of yesteryears began to emerge. Sonal, a Delhi girl, seemed to know a lot of salacious stories and became especially popular during this time. She claimed to have 'experience' in the industry. (I was skeptical of the implications of what that meant.) She spoke of the rumours of 'pageant fixing' in the year Nainika Pradhan had been crowned Miss Indian Beauty. The scandal had very conveniently coincided with Mr Ruia's timely retirement. As the insecurities came forth, the bitching worsened, and I saw it spiralling out of control. I think more than anything, we were scared, scared that this pageant *was* indeed fixed. I was scared too, maybe more than anyone else there. I was not scared of losing, but I was scared that all my hopes and dreams would be harshly shattered. I could deal with losing the competition in a legit, fair fashion, but to have gone through the entire process, taken the great opportunity cost (said the economics major in me), not to mention the risk to my reputation, to find out that there was never any hope to begin with would have been truly awful. All this talk led us to question the integrity of the organizers. All twenty-three of us had followed strict instructions and been at the lobby of the Grand Hotel at 7 a.m., without exception. We had been present with no concessions made for illnesses, family, work or school, and it was just not fair that one contestant was being given the liberty of arriving late. Also, the fact that Indira was a top model with close connections to *Maiden* magazine (one of the magazines owned by the Glamour Group, the cover of which she had appeared on several times) just made the situation even worse.

What was to follow will probably go down in the history of the Miss Indian Beauty pageant. As the gossip trickled down the hallway of the tenth floor, more and more people got wind of what was going on. A few of the feistier ones got together and resolved to get to the bottom of the issue once and for all. There were three of us leading this mini-agitation, and it was interesting to see that the people who were the most involved, and were the force behind this, had received a higher degree of education than the rest. I, being the idealist of the lot, was the leader. Juhi, who was the loudspeaker of the group, was probably a part of this because she sought to be the centre of attention in every situation. And there was Mrinalini. Kalli, as we called her, was a genuinely sweet girl. She was the other one in the group (me being the first) who came with the excess baggage of an accent. She had spent the first ten years of her life in Vijaywada, Andhra Pradesh, and then moved to Auckland, New Zealand, where she now lived. Fame and stardom had lured her back to India, and winning the Miss Indian Beauty crown was to be her first step in that direction. Kalli had been at the fringes of fame in New Zealand, working as a newsreader on one of the more popular TV channels. By virtue of her participation in the Miss Beautiful New Zealand pageant she had recently been offered a few roles in Tollywood, but had decided to take the big step into the limelight and finally aim for stardom through the Miss Indian Beauty pageant. She was very curvaceous, perhaps a bit too curvaceous for the likes of this competition, and could afford to lose a few pounds. Kalli had an ordinary face of the type that one might see at any street corner. She had a no-nonsense sense of style, and dressed in clothes that any trendy twenty-year-old would wear. She was desperate to win this crown, and the thought that this pageant was perhaps fixed terrified her as well. This was probably what drove her to be a part of our agitation.

The three of us decided that the only way to resolve this issue was to get the other twenty involved, frame a letter addressed to Mr Parek expressing our concern over the issue, and have every contestant sign the letter. I, for one, felt that as a contestant in this pageant, I had every right to make my concerns known. This was the idealist in me, raised in a family that encouraged free thinking and education. It was in situations like these that I saw—really saw—the differences in all the girls. Girls such as Harbjeet from Patna and Shrutha from Assam, who had lived sheltered lives—from their parents' homes they would move to their husbands' homes—they went through school, trained to think in rigid boundaries and never go beyond that. Dynamism and rebellion, even for a legit cause, scared them. These girls were used to taking instructions, because that is the way they had survived

73

all their lives, and it was no different now. On the other hand the girls who had experienced education and independence had the capability of taking a view and forming informed opinions.

We were all apprehensive about framing this letter, and were naturally unsure of the results of the actions we were about to take. What happened next sparked a wildfire that spread though the entire group. As we sat together scheming, trying to figure out the best way to spread the word to the group, Juhi (who I really could not stand, but for social purposes stayed on good terms with) came storming into the room, spewing anger. She was so overcome with rage that she had temporarily lost all control of the little English she knew and spurted out fiery broken sentences, which included some rather harsh Hindi and Punjabi words. This is what she had to say. Her brother, who was a model coordinator (I imagined him in my mind, a slimy guy with big biceps, gelled hair, a tight black t-shirt and tight jeans, on his motorbike, hunting out 'models' in the marketplaces of Delhi), had called up Indira's agent to book her for a show. The agent had informed him that Indira was in Dubai for a fashion show. He then went ahead to say that Indira was running for the Miss Indian Beauty pageant, and after the pageant (since he was *so* sure that she was going to win), she would be increasing her show rate by a minimum of Rs 7000. At this point, all our apprehensions dissolved and we decided to bring the entire group together.

In a way all of this was kind of exciting, the juicy gossip, the politics, the rage, the frenzy, the ensuing nervousness. I was enjoying it in an almost sadistic kind of a way. We called up all the twelve rooms on the tenth floor to organize a congregation in my room. The girls came in looking bewildered yet curious, in their night-time outfits. (Can you believe some of them had even organized 'bedtime outfits'?) Many girls had pasty 'whitening' masks on and had oiled their hair to such an extent that it was difficult to look at them without squinting from the shine. While Juhi spewed fire to the group, Mrinalini and I began framing the letter addressed to Mr Parek which we were all to sign.

Mrinalini and I left the room to print out the letter in the business centre. I felt like a true leader, sparking a rebellion for rightful justice. We had cast away our differences and come together to fight the injustice and unfairness of it all, to fight the system that had brought us all together. I was risking it all in the name of honour and integrity. I expelled all fears of getting booted out of the pageant on account of my rebellion. I had to think about the cause. Justice! Integrity! Honour! I imagined myself leading an army of beauty queens—young, beautiful girls riding white horses, wearing sparkling evening gowns, sashes and tiaras, riding through thick fire, in fierce battle with Mr Parek and all his cronies. It was us against the system.

I was quickly jolted out of my quixotic reverie, as when

Mrinalini and I returned, the room was empty. The party had been disbanded. We found out that a puzzled Sonal had walked into the room, astonished to find twenty-one contestants in a state of frenzy. On seeing Sonal many of the girls literally ran out of the room in fear of being tagged as 'rebels'. All the heat and fire of a few moments ago was extinguished in just a few seconds. So much for our uprising. We realized that we had lost our precious chance to get the letter signed. In this moment of desperation, Mrinalini and I went from door to door in a vain attempt to get it signed, but we were met by scared, nervous faces. Many had to 'consult their father or mother', or their 'agent', or whoever. A few girls did agree to sign the letter, and therefore at that moment we were able to distinguish the strong from the weak, those who had a mind of their own and a sense of justice from those who had never been exposed to such ideas. The truth of the matter was that in the letter we hadn't stated anything that was false, harsh, or unjust. We had merely stated the facts as they appeared to us, and all we wanted was some sort of an explanation. How *could* they possibly except us to sit back and accept such open discrimination? Did they really expect us to just sit and watch like dummies, with not even a squeak of protest?

Ultimately, because so many girls refused to sign the letter, we decided to slip it under Sonal's door with no individual signatures, simply signed 'The contestants of the Miss Indian Beauty pageant.' Of course, this being bimboland, the letter was slipped under the wrong door, but we finally got it under the right door and the letter reached who it was meant for.

The next morning when we went down to breakfast, there was strange, sombre, almost nervous feeling in the air. As the day went by we did not hear anything about this affair, and none of us spoke about it. It was like a silent pact between us all that there would be no talk of that night's happenings. There was no point in discussing it, or even thinking about it. We had done what we thought was right, and to look back now would be futile. As the day progressed, it seemed as if everyone had forgotten about the episode.

One fine evening it so happened that Miriam and I were the first ones down for dinner. Sonal and the rest of the Miss Indian Beauty team (as they liked to call themselves) were sitting together engaged in intense conversation. The popular *It's the time to disco* ringtone pierced the air. Sonal picked up her phone. 'Hi Indira, how are you? After discussions we have decided that it is best that you refrain from participating in the contest. No problem, bye.' I thought I saw Sonal smile across the room at me. It was definitely not the most genial smile I have received.

I guess all's well that ends well. I was content with the fact that at least in the eyes of Mr Parek and the rest of the Miss Indian Beauty team, we were no longer a group of spineless beauty queen aspirants. This incident had proved that some of us did have a brain underneath all the make-up.

Clique concept

It was interesting to examine the social formations that were taking place within the group. On closer inspection one could tell that it wasn't random—the cliques that were starting to form were driven by complex social factors.

The group could be divided into three factions—the 'cool' group, the 'desi crew' and the 'freelancers'. As our body clocks adjusted to the new schedule and our bowel movements regularized, we grew closer to each other and hesitatingly wandered away from the safety of our roommates. We discovered that even though we were all vying for the same crown, it was possible to establish cordial and lasting relationships. We were all in this media hell together, and we wanted to have a good time while it lasted.

Most of us were closest to our roommates, so naturally, groups of roommates came together to form cliques, and common threads could be found connecting the individuals in each group. The female of any given species is the more complex animal, as she tends to migrate to social units that match her temperament and behavioural cycles. A similar pattern was observed at the Miss Indian Beauty pageant, as we drifted towards girls with whom we were on the same wavelength.

The 'cool' group, as I called it for lack of a better word, comprised of girls who had been through a wider set of experiences. These included living abroad and/or extensive travel, which lent them not only a broader perspective on life but a more cosmopolitan air. Also, they had a better sense of style. From day one we sensed who our comrades were, and the foundations of the clique were thus laid. The core group included Mrinalini, who had been living in New Zealand for the past ten years, Sonia, her roommate who was a Delhi girl with a great sense of style, which along with her seemingly laid-back nature was her key to entry into the clan, and Juhi, the most aggressive of the group. She talked to everyone, and though we were intimidated by her rather brash nature, she was usually the first to break the ice with everyone.

Then there was Aashima, who lived in Bangkok and had studied in Australia. I failed to understand why Juhi and Aashima came to be such good friends, but for some strange reason they were superglued at the hip. This was her pass for entry into the group. Then there was Miriam and me, for obvious reasons.

A later surprise entry into the group was Stephanie. Stephanie was originally from Goa, but was now living in Andheri, and her claim to fame was winning the Miss Beautiful Mumbai contest. She was a part-time model, actress, hair stylist and fashion designer, and dabbled in anything even remotely related to fashion.

Steph had a cute face with big, round, twinkling eyes, short, curly hair, an upturned nose, and a sweet, yet still seductive smile. She was on the shorter side, but had a good body—thin and rounded in just the right places. I was to become quite close to Steph in the days to come. I was a fan of her carefree nature and her wacky but presentable sense of style. She would couple a pair of cigarette pants with a bright polka-dot shirt, and add clunky jewellery and a cute pair of red shoes to make the outfit come alive. Over the course of the month she became the personal stylist for the group, giving us jewellery to wear for some shoot or the other, or tear up our very plain 'Miss Indian Beauty publicity tees' as I called them, to give them a trendy look. Even though we had professional stylists for all our shoots, we all turned to Steph in moments of need. I grew to like her for what she was, free-spirited and rebellious in that naughty sort of way. But beneath this facade I could see that this was a girl who desperately wanted to win the crown. Did she stand a chance? I seriously doubted it. She was a cute girl, who might have done well in bubbly commercials, but I couldn't really see her representing the country at the international level. Because anything could happen in this contest, I could see her as a potential Miss Earthly Beauty, but she was definitely not a Miss World Beauty or Miss Universal Beauty contender.

As soon as Stephanie noticed who the 'cool' bunch were, she started making obvious attempts at entering the group. To be perfectly honest, we were no exclusive group and it did not take too much (or anything at all, really) to be a part of our clique. Steph played her cards right and soon found herself an integral part of the cool bunch.

And then there was the 'desi' crew. The word desi in this context is probably better described as 'filmi'. Most of the girls who belonged to this category were those whose primary mission in life was Bollywood. A large majority of these girls were either already from Mumbai, or had moved to the locality of Lokhandwala, Mumbai's haven for struggling actors. This was the category of girls who, unlike me, did not want to be Miss Indian Beauty just for the sake of being Miss Indian Beauty. In the same way that I would one day go to business school to further my career, these girls would use this pageant as a stepping stone to get into films. For them the Miss Indian Beauty pageant was clearly the obvious first step in the right direction. It was the desi crew who truly benefited from the intensive training program we were under, and who enjoyed the ride every step of the way—the music videos, the press conferences, the interviews, and the reality TV show.

There were primarily six girls who were part of this crew. Aparita was the youngest of the lot (but had the biggest cup-size). Aparita embodied filmi. From her every expression to her every thrust, this girl was here to make it big in the movies. She was already a fairly successful soap actress, and Miss Indian Beauty was to be her next step to stardom. She really had the most magnificent bust I had ever laid eyes on. Aparita was attractive in a bubbly sort of way, with a pretty but not exceedingly glamorous or beautiful face. She had some serious work to do on her body. She was a tall girl, standing at 5' 9", but she was flabby. Her height and her bravura bust camouflaged her body well, but in a swimsuit all was only too well revealed. Aparita epitomized Bollywood: she breathed, drank, slept and lived it. She woke up in the morning and, in the same way that I read the newspapers, she would open up the celebrity gossip pages and turn on MTV. She woke up to SRK, snoozed to Hrithik, and went to sleep to Salman.

Next was Komal, a Bollywood aspirant who unfortunately had not seen too much success in the world of Bollywood, but was hell-bent on making it. This was Komal's second time in the pageant. She regarded herself as a beauty pageant veteran, and had developed something of a fan following, as girls looked to her for advice. Once when I asked her why she chose to run a second time, she said, 'The first time round, two years ago, I was just a small-town girl with *no* idea of what the world of fashion was about. Over the past two years I have groomed myself, and now I have a better chance at winning the crown.' In the world of Miss Indian Beauty people often use the word 'groom', but I fail to understand the use of this word. I always associate the word 'groom' with the process that my dog undergoes every ten days. I never figured out how the word began to be used in connection with aspiring beauty queens.

The remaining members of the desi crew were Neelam, Poonam and Shanaz. All three of them had careers as 'ad girls'. They were not really model material, as they were short, pretty and chirpy girls. Now and again I see them on television, giggling and preening on some tea, shampoo, or skin-cream commercial.

The 'freelancers' were the most interesting in the cast of characters. There were seven main players in this category, which could be further divided into two. This was the bunch that none of us really understood. I always believed that their quietness could be directly translated into 'seriousness'. The key players of this group were Amisha, Prachi and Preeti. I am not trying to say that these girls were bitchy, because they were not, not in the least bit, but they were solitary creatures. The members of this group would spend much of their time reading their beauty pageant question books and taking the pageant stuff really seriously. These were the girls who wanted the crown the most, and they were going to put in their 200 per cent. While the rest of us saw the training period as a mandatory but somewhat frivolous exercise, they took each day almost as seriously as the finale itself. They reminded me somewhat of those annoying girls in school who always took the front seats, raised their hands for every answer and were shameless teachers' pets.

Amisha was an interesting personality. At the age of twenty-three she had done her degree in fashion designing from a local college in Pune, and was passing her time participating in local fashion shows, starring in a few random Punjabi music videos, and also did some small-time clothes designing. She was a small-town girl who had the fervour to learn, and the desire move on to bigger and better places. She had a pretty face, and was not really a classic beauty, but pretty in that Aishwarya Rai-ish way, with pale skin, light eyes, and pouty pink lips. She had the sort of face that becomes less attractive the more you look at it. While at first glance she appeared beautiful, the more you saw her, the less attractive she became. But I have a peculiar taste in beauty, and I have to say that there was something in that face which I found quite attractive. I think it was the quiet, thoughtful facade that she projected along with her doe-like features which made her appealing in a touch-me-not kind of way. Amisha stood at 5' 7" and did not have a spectacular body by any stretch of the imagination. She had the type of body that one could tell wasn't naturally slender, but had been worked on for hours at the gym to attain a sculpted look. I thought she had a decent body until I saw her in a swimsuit. Beneath the seemingly toned appearance lay thunder thighs and a once-chubby girl who had worked her ass off at the gym to reach this far. All of us had one line or phrase about ourselves that we were to repeat incessantly throughout the month for the benefit of reporters and journalists. The one phrase that I recall Amisha saying was 'I am a fashion designer and stylist by profession and by nature.' I would add a few words to this line each time I heard this, 'Fashion designer and stylist with a bad sense of style', and then chuckle to myself. Amisha was cordial to everyone but was surrounded by a pensive, distant air. Could she win the crown? Well . . . she had a good command over the English language and a pretty face, which could look quite glamorous with make-up. Most of all, she wanted this, she needed this quite badly.

We called the others in this group the 'Miss Congenialities'. The three key members were Harbjeet, Vasundra and Vandana. These three dripped sweetness to a whole new level. I would describe this group as non-threatening and amiable. Their congenial nature arose from their simplicity. They were uncomplicated girls from modest families with simple lives and dreams. I never saw these girls grumble or whine even in the most cumbersome situations, never saw them angry or bitter and, most importantly, I never heard them talk about winning or losing. They were the quiet figures lurking in the background, who made their presence felt only by their considerate and thoughtful nature.

Public display

Some time into our training program we were told that we were to be 'presented' to the press. This was to be our 'coming out' fashion show. This was quite an exciting prospect for us all, especially girls like me who had never walked the ramp for real, with lights, camera and action. Also, this was the very first time I was going to get my make-up and hair done by a professional. This was all quite intimidating for me, because I had only just broken into my heels and was hardly graceful on the ramp.

Due to the miserable organization of the entire proceedings, we were given only two days' notice in advance of the forthcoming press conference. To make things worse, we were informed a day before the event that the designer for the show had flaked out and we would have to arrange for our own outfits, which were to be plain black cocktail dresses. Not all of us had plain black cocktail dresses and black shoes, so we had to help each other out as contact with the outside world was forbidden. We had to work together to figure out outfits for everyone—tops, skirts and even bras were traded to complete outfits. I was pleasantly surprised by how helpful everyone was. I had imagined catfights, sabotaged outfits, and other such horrors, but it was heartening to see twenty-three girls, all contending for the same crown, coming together to help each other out in their hour of need. We actually did quite well and, at the end of it all, only one girl was left without a black skirt. Yasmeen then pitched in to help and offered to lend her a black skirt of her own.

For me, the press conference felt like a bigger deal than the finale itself. How would it feel, I wondered, to be out there under the spotlight, to have cameras flashing and people clapping? Ever since I was a little girl, I had dreamt of this. I would picture myself walking down the ramp, oh-so-tall and skinny and fashionable. And now it was finally happening. I had imagined it would feel different, maybe it had all happened so quickly that I did not have enough time to digest it all. I had imagined it would be so glamorous, but for some reason it felt a tad bit corny. I had not been in front of a big crowd since my high school debating days, and now here I was, all dolled up, strutting down a ramp in three-inch heels. I just hoped and prayed that I wouldn't completely embarrass myself by doing something disastrous, like falling off the ramp.

On the day of the press conference, we all woke up with jitters in our stomach. Yasmeen had psyched us all out about the importance and magnitude of this event, and we all wanted to make a great impression on our first public display. I went down to CG's to await my turn for hair and make-up. The nervousness prevailing in the room was palpable.

The look for the press conference was natural yet elegant. Each one of us sported a very natural, fresh look, which meant lots of petal-pink blush. We had our hair either straightened or in curls. Hair was the simpler part of the process, at least for me, as I have rather manageable ram-rod-straight hair, but make-up was where it got interesting. Prince was our über-cool make-up artist for the event, and we were to interact with him on several occasions. As soon as I laid eyes on Prince, despite his striking, flaming gayness, I had the biggest crush on him, to the extent that I got flustered every time I spoke to him. Prince had brought along a few assistants, one of whom did our Kryolan base, the second who put on our fake eyelashes, and the third who did our body make-up (covering up scars on the knees, stretch marks, etc.) and nails. Prince did the main part of the make-up, which for the Indian face meant primarily the eyes. I was, and still am quite fascinated by the Kryolan phenomenon. Kryolan is a thick, plaster-like make-up base which is used by make-up artists around the world. It stays on for hours, unaffected by the heat of lights, dust, etc. The first thing that came to my mind (this was the economics dork again) when I experienced the Kryolan phenomenon was that whoever manufactured Kryolan must really be raking in the millions, because it had a complete monopoly over the market. It was truly the foundation of any good make-up job.

As I was inexperienced in the art of make-up, the fake eyelash spectacle was a source of great wonder for me. Fake eyelashes really were quite phenomenal, and I was amazed by how they could change the appearance of the entire face for someone like me. In just a flash of a second my tiny, beady, barely discernible eyes were converted into alluring, flirtatious, rather coy instruments of seduction.

After hair and make-up were over for all twenty-three of us, which was really quite an ordeal, we changed into our eclectic range of black cocktail dresses. We were bejewelled in the diamonds provided by our jewellery sponsors, and proceeded to the ballroom—single-file, contestant-number-wise—where the big event was to take place.

By this time, all us were starting to face a range of withdrawal symptoms related to food, which varied from person to person. These symptoms spanned quite a wide range: from chocolate to chicken biryani, to something as simple as a boiled egg. As we passed the buffet lunch which was laid out for the guests, many of the 'healthier' girls stared at the food, their mouths salivating. The ones who were not looking at the food stared at themselves at the mirrors right above the food. It was then that I was to witness the extreme extent of female vanity. While we waited for our grand entry into the ballroom, some girls stood staring at themselves in the mirror above the dessert display, fixing their hair, which was quite in place, touching up their perfect make-up, until at last a waiter told them to move away from the dessert to prevent hair fall into the chocolate mousse.

At long last our moment arrived, and on hearing the music cue, we entered into the lights, flash, and all that jazz, to be shown off to the world as the Miss Indian Beauty contestants for the year. The whole experience was over in a split second. I remember walking in to the jazzy music and waiting for my turn. I heard the presenter announce my name: 'Let's meet Riya, contestant number 7!', saying some cheesy line about me. Then the moment arrived and I walked down the ramp. I strutted and preened as never before, and walked with more razzle and dazzle than I could ever have imagined myself capable of, and at that very instant all the nervousness and apprehension vanished, and for a few seconds I felt like I was on top of the world.

And just like that it was over. My first ramp experience was not as bad as I had expected. When I look back at it now, that was the one and perhaps only walk that I enjoyed, much more than any that were to follow. Maybe it was the novelty of it all, and after the first time, after the shine of newness faded away, I realized the frivolousness and volatile nature of it all. After this one walk, everything that followed became increasingly passé and rather painful.

After all of us had finished our individual ramp walks, we assembled on to the stage and were placed at the mercy of the press, cameras clicking away, smiles plastered on for so long that our faces started to hurt. In the crowd I saw our trainers—Donald, Yasmeen, (I guess Emma was too cool for all this so she did not show up), Mr Parek, and even a few celebrity faces such as the famed artist M.K. Hassan. Later when Mr Hassan was asked what he thought of the present batch, and if he liked any contestant in particular, he was to reply in his customary gruff manner: 'No one, not a single one of them I liked.'

We were soon whisked away to CG's for our lunch, past the colourful buffet that had been set up, past the creamy pastries, the baskets of freshly baked bread rolls, past the steamy, savoury smells, to our bland meal of sprouts and fruit.

In the snap of a finger I had experienced what I had dreamt about for so many years. I was confused. Shouldn't this feel like some glorious achievement? It didn't really feel like that at all. I had fond memories of the experience, I must say, but that was about it. Mostly, it just felt over.

After the taxing press conference we all wanted to go to our rooms to take off the layers of make-up, ready for a much-deserved siesta, but it was not to be. We were told that there was to be a swimsuit shoot for the newly launched entertainment channel, Oomph, and we had to report to the poolside in thirty minutes. I was horror-struck. I was going to be on national television in a swimsuit. This was bad, bad news. Thankfully, several of the other girls felt the same way as I did. Sonal tried to reassure us. 'Girls, don't worry, yaar! The swimsuits are one-piece and you have sarongs!' That didn't help too much. 'OK don't look so scared yaar . . . the concept of the shoot is playful, *innocent* girls—laughing, playing . . . basically, just girls having fun!' We began to feel better. Maybe I could do this after all.

I put on my swimsuit, an ill-fitting piece in a kitschy violet color. I was the last one to get my make-up done, and I was shocked to see the 'look' that the girls were sporting. Dark, garish eye make-up in shades of black, silver and purple, their mouths painted in shades of deep red, hair slicked back, giving them a sleazy, crude look. Shit, I really could not look like this on national TV. What would all the uncles, aunties, buas, mausis, taujis, etc. say?

'Riya, can I talk to you for a minute?' I turned around to see that it was Anjum, a friend of Priya's who had dropped in to watch the Style TV shoot, and was an assistant director with the Oomph crew. 'Sure, dude, what's up?'

'Well. . . . I just thought that I should tell you . . . I shouldn't be . . . but . . . OK, here goes—the show that you are about to shoot for is being directed by the same crew that directs that sex show—*Seduction*. You know . . . the late night show on Oomph?' 'Are you serious?' I exclaimed.

'Yeah, man, I just though that you would like to know . . .'

There was no way I was going to be on *Seduction* in a swimsuit. Oomph had already established quite an infamous reputation, and I really did not want to be a part of this. But honestly, what could I possibly do? Another letter? Another protest? I don't think any of us were ready for that. This group of somewhat spiritless girls were the types who would complain and bitch to each other, but when it came to taking action, there would be silence. There was no way I was willing to be the leader again and establish (if I had not done so already) a reputation as an instigator. I kept shut, and with growing apprehension about the shoot, listened to the complaints surrounding me.

The worst was yet to come. The location of the shoot was the poolside. I was shocked by the tastelessness of the set. There was a divan covered by red satin sheets, a dressing room set with glittery lights, and a bar scene with bubble machines and boas. An assistant came to give us our 'accessories', which were the last straw for me. Our main accessory was a sarong, if you could possibly even call it that, a five-inch-wide cloth of sheer polyester. There were also feather boas in garish pinks and purples, plastic pearls, and gold plastic tiaras. You get the point. I was definitely not going to do this. The thought of my grandmother seeing me on national television as a part of this vulgar show made me feel ill. I was literally faint with worry.

I put all my creative juices to work and cooked up what seemed to be an ingenious plan. I would feign sickness, get my mother to call up Sonal for permission to see our 'family doctor', and get Rushab to pick me up. This way I would not only escape the shoot, but flee the location as well. I was all set to launch my plan into action. But of course, things never really work out as they are planned, especially at the Miss Indian Beauty contest.

I was cut short even before I could try out the plan. I was up in my room, ready for take-off, when I got a phone call. 'Riya, come down immediately.' It was one of our hound-dog chaperones. This called for desperate measures. I invoked the actress in me. I wiped off all my make-up in such a way that mascara streamed down my face, and my eyeliner cast dark circles around my eyes. I truly appeared ill. I went down, dragging my feet, my hair and make-up in a state of chaos. I not only looked, but also felt wretched. I could see that several of the girls were close to tears, ill at ease with the situation but unable to muster up the courage to say or do anything about it. As Prince set about reapplying my make-up, cooing words of comfort, I guzzled an entire bottle of water, and then jumped up from my chair, feigning nausea. Appearing to be in the greatest possible state of human discomfort, I clutched my stomach and throat and threw up while producing a distressing sound. I spewed out water and bits of sprouts. The director of the shoot gave me pitying look. It was working! Step one accomplished. 'Shit, yaar . . . she is really not well . . . we'd better let her take some rest.' The chaperones hurriedly ushered me back to the safety of my room.

Step two of my plan failed miserably. I called my ever-supportive parents and explained to them the dreadful situation that I was in. My mom called Sonal and gave her the family doctor story. Sonal agreed to let me go *but* I had to take a chaperone along. So much for enjoying an evening with Rushab. I racked my brains to find a solution to this problem. There was no escape. I thought I might as well just go to sleep.

By this point Miriam and Stephanie, who were more strong-willed than the rest, began complaining about the vulgarity and inappropriate nature of the shoot. They returned to their rooms angry and frustrated. Sonal and the other organizers were starting to get wind of the situation. I, satisfied that I had solved the situation in the best possible way, was in for an unpleasant surprise. I heard the doorbell ring and opened the door to Sonal and the entire crew of the show. 'Riya, yaar . . . please, do this one for me. Five minutes, I promise, that's it. Each and every contestant has to be on the show, even if it is only for a minute . . . please . . . for me?' She begged and pleaded. What could I possibly have done in this situation but agree. It wasn't like I was on my deathbed!

I went downstairs to get my make-up started again. Prince informed me that this show was titled Miss 10. The concept was this. Viewers could SMS in their votes for their favourite contestant to the number 1010, and the contestant with the highest number of votes would get a wildcard entry into the top ten. I decided that if I did not even have what it takes to make it into the top ten on my own capability, then there was no way that I could win this contest. I put in a half-baked five minute effort to get ready, not even bothering to get my hair done.

I was taken aback by the peculiar-looking crew of the show. After spending two years at an all women's college, it was inevitable that I was to become quite familiar with the notion of lesbianism. Even though I had accepted the idea, and had even become quite comfortable with it (in fact, some of my closest friends were lesbians), it was difficult for me to absorb the fact that it existed here in traditional Indian society. Here, right in front of me, was the notorious production team of *Seduction*—a living example that it did very much exist here. I don't think I have ever come across lesbians who are blatantly open about their choice in India, at least not in the circles that I haunt. At times one does suspect, but it's always hidden away behind closed doors. Here we had a crew full of Indian to-the-core 'dykes', with crew-cuts, caps, torn jeans that sagged to show plaid boxers, big sneakers, the works.

It was quite amusing to see the goings on at the sidelines of the shoot. Twenty girls (minus Miriam, Steph and I) were lying on the grass under the grey Mumbai skies, completely drained of all energy and enthusiasm. The minute they came under the lights of the camera, they momentarily transformed into dancing nymphs, bubbling with energy, throwing seductive looks at the camera. When it was over they would go back and collapse on their moist imprints in the grass.

I went to bed after I had finished the promised five minutes. Slowly but steadily the girls dropped out, gave up, and went to bed. The shoot went on till dawn by the poolside and water fountains. Despite their fatigue and exhaustion, girls were desperately trying to look their best, digging into untapped energy reserves to muster up all they could to make it through the night and try to appear as sexy and appealing as they possibly could. They desperately wanted that wildcard entry to ensure them that spot in the top ten. They looked depressing, surrounded by the boas, the bubble-machine, the Mardi Gras pearls and the plastic tiaras. The plastic tiaras which somehow represented the plastic dreams that each girl held, the plastic dreams that provided each one of them with the energy to go on through the night, posing, posturing, preening.

So who did finally win Miss 1010? It was the one girl who truly deserved it, the one who wanted it the most, and the one that gave it her all, till six in the morning. She was the last one standing, the one who threw the most beguiling looks at the camera, complete with winks, smirks and pouts. It was our very own Sonia, the sweet-looking, boot-wearing, finger-licking-hot chick from Delhi. Sonia came from a typical nouveau riche Delhi family, for whom all the glitz and glamour that came with the crown would have been quite enticing. Winning that crown meant a certain rise on the rungs of the Delhi social ladder.

Sonia had a charming, pretty air about her. A lot of people thought she was hotness personified, but that was probably because of the way she dressed. With that skinny body of hers she could pull off close to anything. Sometimes I really liked the way Sonia dressed—if only she could tone it down a little. She always went all out. Even when the others had toned down, she would inevitably go overboard with the make-up, the jewellery, the boots, the works. Sonia's premier claim to fame was her impressive collection of boots. She owned a pair in every imaginable style and colour.

I tried to picture Sonia's life a few years from now. I envisaged her lying in a pastel-coloured silk robe on a king-size bed (in an ostentatious house), filing her perfectly manicured nails while gossiping with her girlfriends, waiting for her troll-like nouveau riche husband to come home from work. Then she would proceed to get dressed in her diamonds and go off to some party or the other, and socialize the night away. But before Sonia could get that husband, she needed that crown. On the big night she was the very first to find out that she had made it to the top ten; the very same night that I stood at the back, gaping at the top ten.

Sunday blues

We all waited for Sundays with eager anticipation. This was the one day that we were allowed to see our loved ones. Of course, there were rules. Leaving the hotel was undreamt of, we could only have visitors, and that too within a time slot of three hours. We were restrained to the lobby area, where we were monitored by the omnipresent Miss Indian Beauty chaperones. As if having the chaperones keeping a hawk's eye on us wasn't bad enough, we had the Style TV people filming the entire thing as well. They hoped to catch on tape our 'interactions' with our families, as if we were part of a scientific experiment which involved an exotic species of animal.

I must have looked at my watch at least a hundred times on our first Sunday. As I anxiously waited for the clock to strike four-thirty, the designated 'visitors' hour', I constantly daydreamt of the anticipated moment, that moment when I would run into the arms of my beloved. I pictured it as something out of a story book, the captured princess rushing into the arms of her prince. The few minutes that they would have together would fuel her with the courage to face the next one week, until she saw his sweet, loving face again. I would cherish the few minutes I would get with Rushab, taking his slender fingers in my hands, our lips trembling with desire. And then, the evil chaperones would come with their spears and chains to drag the beautiful princess away from her prince, into the dark and dismal confines of that hated dungeon called CG's.

After what seemed like an eternity, though it had only been just about a week, I desperately wanted to see a face that wasn't part of this beauty pageant. Seeing the same faces over and over again, day and night, from sessions to shoots, was starting to get to me, and I was in dire need of a breather. Also, I was very excited about the prospect of my best friend Shreeya coming and 'checking out' the competition. I had been filling her into all the juicy Miss Indian Beauty gossip on the phone, and after my vivid descriptions of my co-competitors, she was excited at the prospect of coming and seeing all the contestants in flesh and blood.

When 4.30 p.m. finally arrived, I kicked off my heels, dove into my flip-flops and rushed to the lobby to find Rushab eagerly waiting for me. He too was quite curious by this point, and wanted to come and check out the 'Miss

Indian Beauty scene'. He had even wanted to bring along a few of his cronies who had picked out their favourites and were hoping to get a sighting, and if very lucky, a conversation, but I had refused. I didn't want to play the part of the pimp. I reassured them that I was developing deep friendships with the 'chicks' and that his friends would get an introduction after the pageant.

Rushab and I strategically chose an inconspicuous corner love seat, and I enforced a strict hands-off rule, which was intensely difficult, considering that we had not seen each other for such a long time. We felt seriously uncomfortable surrounded by the other contestants and their families (who were probably talking about us), the chaperones (or should I say bodyguards), and most annoyingly, Style TV.

By this point, being an avid coffee-drinker, I was going through some serious caffeine-withdrawal symptoms and was in urgent need of an espresso shot. Our in-room dining had been blocked, and this was probably my one and only chance to fulfill my desire. As our order arrived at the table, I slyly placed my cup in front of Rushab and took a big gulp. Sunday was my day of gluttony, and no one, not even our hound-dog chaperones, could stop me. I made Rushab order delicacies such as french fries and onion rings (to satisfy my carbohydrate cravings for the week) and stealthily slipped them off the plate, once again placed tactically in front of Rushab. A french fry never tasted as good as it did on those treasured Sundays.

I must say though, the most enjoyable part of these Sundays was scrutinizing and analyzing each competitor with Shreeya. We would go from the lobby to the coffee shop (the only two places where we were allowed to have visitors), and back again to the lobby, sniffing out contestants, at which point we would find a strategic location to seat ourselves. Shreeya would then put on her sunglasses, stare for a few minutes (at times much longer) and give me her detailed analysis of each girl, after which we would debate several crucial points such as hair and skin, and then eventually arrive at a mutual agreement about her chances at winning the contest.

Throughout that month it was those Sundays that would keep me going. They were a true relief from the chaos surrounding us, which would only increase day by day. At times I could not handle it anymore, the constant chatter about who was going to win, who was getting what 'work', what the best skin-care products were, who the best make-up artists were. I just wanted to escape the constant competition, the relentless scrutiny, and though my mind would never let me completely escape, these sacred Sundays would give me something of a break.

As if having the Style TV people on our backs 24-7, filming

our every move and catching us at out very worst was not bad enough, we now had all sorts of new additions to the media frenzy. Day after day, it was some shoot or the other. From shoots for cellphone companies where we had to record cheesy messages about why we liked to talk on the phone, to shoots wishing the women of India a Happy Women's Day (as we represented the epitome of womanhood), I was completely convinced that this pageant was really just one big publicity stunt. All this was really quite soul-destroying, and took out quite a large chunk of our time and energy. We survived on five hours of sleep (I wonder what happened to beauty sleep), and went through most of our sessions like zombies (especially Emma's sessions). As if the publicity stunts were not bad enough, we had mandatory interviews for various channels, from the local Marathi station to national news stations. The girls from comparatively remote states such as Uttaranchal and Assam got even more attention than the rest from their local channels.

I was amazed at the publicity this pageant was receiving. The Miss Indian Beauty pageant was a big deal, I agreed, but I never imagined it to be such a big deal. It was surreal to be a part of a pageant that I had been seeing on TV for years. I still remember the year that Meeta Sengupta and Alisha Ray won, how I watched the reruns of the pageant over and over again, and now I was going to be one of those girls on TV.

The only thing was that I was still trying to hide the fact

that I was a part of this pageant. I avoided any phone calls
that I would get from family or friends, and tried to remain
as inconspicuous as possible. I always migrated to the
background of any picture or photo shoot, while everyone
pushed for the most coverage and a chance to be in the
limelight. Being a part of the backdrop was unnatural for
me. I was used to being the leader, being in the front line,
but here I would run for cover at the flash of a camera. I
was trying hard, really hard, to be able to immerse myself
in this, but I just could not get myself to do it. I never got
used to the flashes of the camera, no matter how hard I
tried. I had come here with some sort of a crazy ambition
to be a beauty queen who would propagate goodwill, but
I was beginning to realize that this perhaps was not possible.
I thought that the training program was meant to make
each and every one of us fit—mentally and physically, and
to help us perform at our very best on the big night of the
pageant. To my disappointment, the organizers did not really
attempt to do this. In retrospect, I remember my time at
the Miss Indian Beauty pageant more as one big publicity
stunt, with photo shoots, interviews and recordings, rather
than what it was supposedly meant to be, a time for self-
improvement.

In our batch of twenty-three girls, there were eight girls
who came from a 'defence background', as they liked to

put it. Throughout the history of the pageant there had been a large percentage of girls belonging to a defence background who had participated in the pageant, and would very often emerge as winners. Over the years, several army girls had won—Tara Dutt, Priya Chopra, Celine Chandra, Nidhi Kapadia, and Gulpreet Narula among several others.

Why army girls? This could be attributed to a variety of factors. The very first was the genetic factor. The typical army parent is of a build superior to the average Indian man (or woman), as the army has set minimum physical standards for entry. Therefore, army girls usually have a better physique than the average Indian girl. That's one.

Secondly, being in the festive and rather jovial milieu of the army community, attending army schools all their lives, army girls acquire a good grasp of the English language. They also receive good exposure to different situations from the frequent moves that their parents have to make, from one army base to the other across the nation. Naturally, a pretty girl who is raised well wants to move ahead in life. There are two ways of doing this—studying hard, or trying to make it in the entertainment business. Hitting the books is obviously the more boring option, and for a pretty, well-spoken girl, what could be easier than winning the Miss Indian Beauty pageant and being thrust into instant stardom?

An army girl, being well-rounded, good-looking, and with the added advantage of having travelled across the country, has a better chance of doing well in a beauty pageant than say, a pretty girl who's spent all her life in a small town like Nagpur. See, it's actually quite simple. Army girls have it all, looks, personality, etc., but the thing they do not have is money. It's simply human nature—every pretty girl out there wants to be rich and famous, and for a good-looking girl, the entertainment business is the fastest and easiest way to achieve this.

At times I wondered if the selection process of the Miss Indian Beauty pageant was like the American college acceptance process, where the admissions committee tries to assemble a varied group of people representing different states, countries and religions. Unlike the Miss America pageant, where there are fifty contestants representing each one of the states, the Miss Indian Beauty pageant consisted of girls primarily from Delhi, Mumbai or Bangalore. At the Miss Indian Beauty contest, we seemed to have our token Muslim, Christian, Parsi and Gujju participants. Most of the girls had North Indian origins.

Shanaz was our token Muslim from Chennai. She was one of our 'Indian blondes', with a lively and animated personality, but not too much of a head on her dainty shoulders. She was a cute girl, short and thin, with doll-like looks—curly hair, porcelain skin, and beautifully-rounded features. She was lively (sometimes a bit too

107

lively) and had rather disturbing tendencies—she would sometimes take to poking girls in their breasts and bottoms.

Shanaz would go all out with the make-up and flashy outfits. The problem with her, and many of the other girls, was that even though they had cute clothes, shoes and bags, they did not pair them together to form appropriate outfits. Somewhere along the way they would screw it up by wearing a pair of shoes or earrings that just did not complement the look. For example, Shanaz would wear a cute pastel, baby-doll skirt with a plain cotton halter, but then ruin the look by wearing a pair of hot-pink plastic stilettos and jazzy earrings. If she had laid off the heels, and instead worn a simple pair of flip-flops, the outfit would have been charming, but instead a 'wannabe glam' factor came in. Once when I asked her what her career aspirations were, she very confidently replied that she wanted to be a supermodel on the international ramps. Standing at 5' 6", I had no idea how she would manage that. Shanaz was a local model in Chennai, and also emceed shows and parties. She had risen to the highest that she possibly could in Chennai, and had now hit a glass ceiling. Miss Indian Beauty was her entry into the world above that glass ceiling, the world that right now she could only stare up and gape at.

Shrutha hailed from Guwahati, and was our token representative from the North-East. Though I feel bad when I say so, she was the worst of the lot. I could see no reason why she was here. The only reason that I could possibly think of was because she was from the North-East. Shrutha's claim to fame was her five-minute cameo role in the hit movie 'Bollywood', where she played the part of an actress who was sleeping around for roles.

This had to be the corniest idea ever. An 'anthem' for a beauty pageant? As if the Miss Indian Beauty pageant held such gravity and importance. Seriously, it was just a beauty pageant, and that reality needed to be emphasized. We had been informed that a music video was going to be created, with all the contestants in it. I was appalled. As if being part of a reality TV show and being on Page 3 almost daily was not bad enough, now of all things, we would have to be in a music video. Anyway, now that I had to do it, I felt I should keep shut and go along with it. There was no point in creating another scene.

On hearing the word 'music video', an instantaneous alarm went off in my head like a reflex action, and I pictured twenty-three girls clad in outrageous outfits, swaying their hips and gyrating to a vulgar tune. Thankfully, almost as if to redeem for the Oomph incident, this music video was of a completely different nature. The song was titled '*Roop*' and was one of those shrill, sweet, melodramatic Hindi numbers. It spoke of young girls growing up into beautiful, young, talented women, who transformed from simple children in classrooms into the ravishing Miss Indian Beauty contestants that they were today.

Much too early on a Monday morning, we loaded into our beauty mobile and were taken to Kamala Mills, a decrepit set of dilapidated buildings which were a popular location to shoot B-grade movies and music videos. I cannot even begin to explain how unenjoyable this two-day experience was. Any tiny Bollywood hope that I might have had vanished completely. Here we were, bright and early on an extremely hot and humid Monday morning. We clambered into our respective trailers, and one by one, over the course of the next six hours, we were called for hair and make-up, and then proceeded to shoot our bit in the music video.

The concept of the music video was supposed to be very young and fresh. We dressed in bright, colourful outfits in oranges, blues and yellows which complemented the look. We each had about a two second role in the video, as there were twenty-three of us and the video was only three minutes long. We were clicked holding up our baby pictures, jumping on trampolines, throwing around beach balls, sitting in a classroom, things of that nature. But twenty-three was a whole lot of girls, and just two seconds on camera call for at least an hour of shooting, so we had to do about twenty-three hours of shooting in total.

We waited around, trapped in our uncomfortable

make-up vans, which we were forbidden to leave so that we would not get a tan. We complained away to glory as we sat munching on the fruits and nuts which had been brought along as snacks. As we whiled away the time, attempts were made at practicing for the Q&A round from the book that we had each been given. To top it all off, my cellphone's battery ran out. Here I was, in what felt like the middle of nowhere, cut off from all contact with the outside world. The only solace I found in the hours that followed was writing in my journal, an activity that I had recently found to be cathartic. Also, I felt like this experience had to be documented. The unlimited cups of syrupy sweet cutting chai that were provided at the set were perhaps the only inspiration to get through those two awful days. By this point, even our hound-dog chaperones did not have the courage to stop us from drinking these illegal cuppas of chai. How I cherished those cups of tea. Each sip that I took from those tiny, sticky cups, half-full with thick, steaming liquid, the thin star-shaped layer of malai already forming on the surface, was truly divine.

Another source of excitement that materialized during those two grey, dreary days were the sandwiches that we were given for lunch. After having been deprived of bread for close to two weeks now, the effect of a slice of bread, even though it was a funny wholegrain variety, was glorious. Even though the sandwiches featured just a layer of lime-coloured chutney, a few sprouts, a single cucumber, and if

111

we were lucky, a slice of tomato, and would have been unsavoury under normal circumstances, at that moment in time seemed to be the most scrumptious delicacy on the face of the earth. I was quite taken aback to see some of the scrawniest girls chow down five sandwiches, and even more surprised when I myself gobbled down three.

To my great dismay, Prince wasn't our make-up artist for this event, and had been replaced by a guy named Kapoor. There had been some controversy regarding our make-up, and now we were testing out new make-up artists.

We proceeded to shoot our bits, and at sundown, due to technical reasons of lighting, we had to stop shooting. We then piled into the waiting queue of Toyota Qualises, contestant-number-wise, ready to go back to the hotel. Even after an extremely taxing day of shooting, many girls were distressed that they had received less film time than the others. Some even went to the extent of complaining of partiality by the director. Because of this, we were called back for yet another day of shooting. I felt like I had been shot, and went back to the hotel feeling injured and bruised, as if I had fought a hard battle, singing our very own beauty anthem quietly to myself.

Mid-life crisis

Almost exactly halfway through the training period, two weeks down, but with more than ten days to go, all of us suffered a 'mid-life crisis'. At this point, each of us started feeling the strain of the past two weeks of activity, and the stress of the upcoming pageant. There was a certain lull and apathy that was present at all the events. Feeling the effects of all the stress and pressure, we missed our homes, families, and most of all, our own comfortable beds.

By this time we were all fed up of the satwik diet, and were craving the simple things in life such as eggs, bread and milk. The non-vegetarians of the group were yearning for chicken. The cravings got so strong that some girls resorted to desperate measures. As is the norm in hotel rooms, our rooms too were supplied with complimentary tea and coffee. Therefore each one of us had an infinite supply of tea bags, coffee sachets, dairy creamer and pouches of

sugar. Several of the girls started carrying around pouches
of dairy creamer and sugar in their pockets and bags, and at
regular intervals, much like one would do with tic-tacs or
breathsavers, would devour the contents of the packet. As
CG's (very annoyingly) did not have a dustbin, at the end
of each day we would see empty packets of dairy creamer
and sugar scattered in the corners. Once Sonal and her
crew got wind of the situation, housekeeping was instructed
to remove all tea/coffee supplies from the rooms.

Some of us went to even greater extremes, telling our
friends and families (in most cases boyfriends) to drop off
packets of food at the reception, taking the great risk of
getting caught. One day, under the stress of it all, I too felt
the need for some fried, feel-good food, and so Rushab
delivered a big bag of McDonalds stuff for me and all my
friends, complete with milkshakes, french fries and chicken
nuggets. Several of the girls (who did not have family or
friends in the area) went to the extent of bribing the
housekeeping staff to purchase chocolates and cigarettes
for them.

Smoking was absolutely banned, and we had a few
smokers in our group, my roommate being one of them.
Honestly, how can you stop someone who's been smoking
for the past five years to quit at the snap of a finger, and that
too for twenty-five of perhaps the most stressful days of
her life? Under the strain, many girls resorted to closet
smoking, though not exactly in the closet, but in the

bathroom. Someone, out of fear of getting caught, invented an ingenious way of concealing the stench of cigarette smoke. It was discovered that it was possible to smoke a safe cigarette by letting a hot shower run for a few minutes, following which the bathroom would steam up, and the steam would clear away the stale reek of cigarette smoke. After that discovery it became difficult for me to find a moment to shower, as Miriam was constantly in the bathroom. After all, the bathroom is a fun place to pass time anyway, and offers many amusing activities such as popping pimples, picking at blackheads, hair removal, and now, to add to the list, smoking.

At this point our training sessions were disturbingly underattended and completely drained of energy. A majority of the girls were upstairs in their rooms and claimed to be faced with some ailment or the other, be it runny eyes, swollen ankles, and in several cases, 'weakness' or 'fever'. In addition to this, many of the girls who were attending the sessions claimed to be feeling dizzy or faint. I would have been the first to go up to my room and chill with some excuse or the other, but I felt I had done my bit of feigning illness for the month, and could not really afford to do it again.

During this time we went through some rather touching moments of girl bonding. During a Q&A session with Yasmeen, Harbjeet, deprived of sleep and chicken, broke down when asked a particularly tough question that she could not answer. This in turn led to a chain reaction of tears, and for that one moment we all indulged in glorious self-pity and found comfort in each others' presence and pain.

In this dismal phase, when spirits were at an all time low, with neither novelty nor adrenaline to fuel us, Mr Parek blessed us with his presence in the hope of motivating us to survive the next ten days with zest and enthusiasm. He reiterated the fact that this was a life-changing experience and a once-in-a-lifetime opportunity, so we must all put in our 200 per cent. Though this was quite easy to say, it was much more difficult to execute, especially under the mounting pressure and sleep-debt that we were accumulating. Fortunately, this stage was not to last for very long, as the one-week mark brought with it a fresh rush of adrenaline and anxiety that only increased through the course of that week.

Well . . . I can't exactly call it freedom, but that's pretty much what it felt like when for the first time in ten days we stepped outside our hotel and felt the fresh evening air whisk through our blow-dried hair. Never had the din of Mumbai traffic sounded so peaceful, or the carbon fumes smelt so sweet. I raised my arms up to the sky and took it all in, the blue-grey of the sky, the silhouette of the emerging moon, and the occasional buzzing of a helicopter carrying some CEO or the other far above the crazy Mumbai traffic to the safety of his home.

This was the first time in ten days that we were to step out of the security of our hotel into the concrete jungle of Mumbai. It had never been so exciting. Even though we were only headed to Coffee Bean Cafe, a chain of coffee shops sponsoring another one of our many publicity stunts, it felt great. All twenty-three faces were aglow with delight. Going to a coffee shop had never been so thrilling, even though we were not to be served any coffee. We were all just so glad to be stepping out into the real world.

Coffee Bean Cafe had launched a publicity scheme by which the general public would get the chance to ask one of the finalists a question on the big night in lieu of a judge. Each table at the outlet had little plastic boxes, in which people could propose potential questions. The person with the winning question would receive a diamond crown for their efforts, along with the chance of asking the chosen question.

I don't think I have ever seen anyone so dressed up to go to a coffee shop. We were all wearing the white Miss Indian Beauty t-shirts that we had been given. Steph, the self-proclaimed stylist of the group, had 'styled' them for us, tearing up the bottoms, or ripping off a shoulder or neckline to make these rather plain t-shirts appear quite cool. The simplicity of these t-shirts didn't stop the girls from dolling up; in fact, it only inspired them to deck up even more. Girls sported racy stilettos and trendy boots along with teensy-weensy skirts, or wore buttock-hugging hipster jeans. Let me not forget the jewellery that many of the girls had donned, from dangling, glittering chandelier earrings to chunky plastic hoops. I too had tried, putting on a pair of neon-pink three-inch heels and wearing my tightest jeans, but I still felt out of place among the group as I just could not get myself to plaster on the make-up for a visit to Coffee Bean Cafe. Along with my body, my skin too needed a breath of fresh air.

We all loaded into our Miss Indian Beauty mobile, the bright pink luxury bus festooned with banners advertising the pageant, which had become our constant companion on our travels. It screamed the sponsor's Fresh! slogan and the rather thoughtless Miss Indian Beauty line of 'Be the most beautiful girl in the world'. When we arrived at our destination we were made to wait inside the bus. I stared out of the window sceptically to see what was happening at Coffee Bean Cafe. There were a few cameras lined up at the entrance, most of which belonged to the Style TV people, and a few customers sat outside sipping their mugs of coffee, looking rather disinterested in the goings-on. We stepped out of the bus into our seats at Coffee Bean Cafe, which were in a claustrophobic enclosure which had been specially created for us. There were some apathetic stares and some mild applause. The radio jockey who had been hired to cover the event tried to stimulate some excitement amidst the crowd, with no success, as I crouched in the corner trying to hide myself from the eye of the camera. I had no desire to be part of this cheesy event. The annoying RJ tried to prompt the crowd to pose questions for the contestants, but no one seemed interested. Finally, an awkward, pimply teenager stood up and posed an inane question. 'If you had to break up with your boyfriend, what would you do?' He got equally ridiculous answers from some of the contestants, who were growing increasingly desperate for camera time. We were asked other questions such as 'What's the best way to propose to a girl?' and 'What do you look for in a boyfriend?' I was quite embarrassed by this entire situation, as girls fought to be the centre of attention by answering these silly questions, the pimply adolescents enjoying all the attention thoroughly. I refused to be a part of any of this and slouched in my chair, wishing I could be wiped off the face of this earth, all the while taking in the divine aroma of the coffee that I wasn't allowed to have.

The most exciting moment of this entire trip was when the waiters brought out the snacks, which comprised of fruit (of course) and pasta salad, which we all happily devoured. To top off these delicacies we were served the 'Miss Indian Beauty drink'. Coffee Bean Cafe had created a 'beauty potion' for the pageant, which was essentially a strawberry milkshake doused with strawberry syrup and layers of whipped cream. We couldn't believe our eyes when we were served this drink. It was hardly the healthiest drink for beauty pageant aspirants. As expected, our chaperones snatched the drinks away from us, much like one takes candy away from a naughty child, and we stared longingly at the drinks that were so cruelly taken away from under our noses.

That was the end of our thrilling evening. A few rather senseless questions, a sip of strawberry shake, an exciting pasta salad, and we were on our way back to the confines of our hotel.

On the way back I stared out on to the streets of the city and marvelled at the lights, the signs, the colours, the people swarming like ants everywhere, on their bikes, in their cars, on foot. I stared out at the line of slums that we passed and saw happy families assembled on cots set underneath flimsy tin roofs, staring into the bright lights of their television sets. I saw beggars staring curiously at the smiling faces adorning the banners on our beauty mobile, and gazing up higher to see the profiles of laughing, smiling faces, caked with bright make-up. It was such a bizarre world that I was a part of.

Throughout the course of the pageant, the dreamy side of me was battling with the solid, rigid side of me that years of education and hard work had created. I had wanted to be a Miss Indian Beauty ever since I was a little girl, but for me it had been a whim that I had finally mustered up the courage to execute. I knew that if I won, it would be an exciting experience, and I would get the fame that I had been yearning for. It would be nice to be on Page 3 once in a while, to be invited to cool parties and what not, but really, that was all I expected out of this. I realized that I would eventually go back to my old life, because that was me. The sad part was that these girls expected this experience to be life-changing. They expected the contest to pave the way for the beginning of the rest of their lives. They did not realize that all this was not real, and the goal that they had been working towards for years and years was just a facade. They would realize it, just as I did—they had to—but when and how, only time would tell.

I gazed down from my seat at the flurry of activity taking place on the streets below me and listened to the sounds of the city, oblivious to the screeches and screams of the girls as they played a noisy round of Antakshari. As the dark towers of our hotel loomed up before us, I was jolted back to reality. We were back to our plush, carpeted surroundings, away from the heat, dust and laughter of the outside world. As I stepped into the lobby from the sticky heat of the outdoors into the cool blast of the A.C., I was whisked back into the world of beauty pageants, where everything can appear as beautiful as you want it to be.

Spirituality for success

One night, as we walked towards our rooms, exhausted after a full day of activity, we were told to change into 'comfortable clothing' and be down in five minutes. Donald was about to undertake a 'meditation and relaxation session' by the pool. Despite my fatigue I was eager to attend this session, being an avid fan of meditation techniques. A meditation session was indeed a good idea to relieve us of the stress and anxiety that was starting to build up. I was expecting something along the lines of 'Om' chanting, and perhaps a bit of relaxing yoga to calming music, but what we got was something quite unexpected.

We all gathered around the poolside, which was quite the perfect setting for a meditation session. The pool was located on the top floor of the hotel, and gave a panoramic view of twinkling city lights and the vast expanse of the ocean. The pool was bordered with candles, and the water sparkled with the light of even more floating candles, and was literally covered with red rose petals. We were enchanted by the scene that had been created, and only realized why and by whom this had been done when the Style TV people walked in with their lights and cameras. Naturally, where there was Donald, there would inevitably follow a camera.

What happened next was mentally exercising for us in more ways than one. We were made to sit in a circle, each one of us with a candle in front of us, staring into the eyes of a cameraman who was submerged in the pool amidst the rose petals and the candles, with a camera mounted on his shoulder.

We shut our eyes and then Donald began. 'Imagine yourself on the Miss Indian Beauty stage . . . Each one of you dressed in a beautiful designer outfit made especially for you, the Windsor diamonds you are wearing glittering in the lights. Picture yourself walking down that ramp, a smile on your face . . . You are confident in every way, graceful and poised.' He paused and some background music went off. We heard the cameraman moving around in the water. Then a splash and 'Oh Shit!'. Donald continued, 'Imagine the hosts calling out ten names, ten names chosen by God, by destiny, to be asked those ten questions . . . Your name is called in that ten . . . see yourself glowing with happiness.' We heard the camera crew swilling around in the pool, and a few more plunks in the water. 'Picture

123

yourself giving perfect answers, answers that lay within you, to questions that you know so well. Then you go backstage, and emerge in the lights in even more opulent outfits, waiting for the top five to be announced . . . Once again your name is called out, the dream that lies within you, slowly unfolding into reality . . . Now, picture yourself walking down that stage, to the podium where you will be writing out your answers. Each one of you is calm, collected, beautiful and resplendent with the glow of confidence . . . Then you listen, listen carefully and completely to the common question, after which you each pen down your answer, your flawless answer.'

At this point, I thought I heard some sobs. I opened my eyes to see three more cameramen in the pool. I was rather bored by this whole scene by now, and really could not understand how this was supposed to be calming.

'You put down your pens and wait, wait with tranquility, for the three names, the names that have been chosen, not by the judges, but by God himself, names that had been chosen long, long ago, names that had already been penned down in the books of destiny . . . The three names are called out with great aplomb and applause, the second runner-up, the first runner-up, and then the Miss Indian Beauty, the title that you are all vying for. As you stand there, resplendent in your outfit designed especially for you by Manish Kumar, you pray and hope that you are the chosen one, the one destined to win that crown.'

I heard some deep breathing around me.

'You wait with anticipation and eagerness, composed and relaxed. Finally, the name is called out, *The Miss Indian Beauty for this year is* . . .' At this point, disbelievingly, I heard every single girl around me screech out her name as loudly as she possibly could. Twenty-two names which echoed through my mind again and again, till they slowly faded away. Then silence.

I opened my eyes and looked around, and was surprised to see tears glittering in several eyes.

The power of love

Ten out of the twenty-three of us had boyfriends, and of these ten, five girls had boyfriends who were in Mumbai, including myself. We were all ill at ease with the fact that we were not able to spend quality time with our boys, free from the eyes of the camera and chaperones. We did meet our boyfriends on Sundays, and on these cherished days, to satisfy our innate desires we would hold hands under the table and play some very intense games of footsie. By week two I could bear it no longer, especially as Rushab lived right around the corner. It was quite exasperating that I was in Mumbai for an entire month and I could not see him when he was just a five-minute drive away. At some point or the other through the training period each of us gave in to the power of love and came up with some rather creative ways to satisfy our yearnings.

From the very day that I learnt about the countless

restrictions, I began searching for methods of escape. After extensive research and some rather ingenious planning, I had finally come up with a conceivable plan of action, and by the beginning of week three I was desperate enough to go through with it. I wanted to be with Rushab, alone, even if it was just for a few precious moments. I wanted to let go of all inhibitions and break free from the constant surveillance. I had a mission, and I was all set to go out there, quite literally, to accomplish it.

I came upon an escape plan quite by chance. One day, while I was on the phone, having a conversation with my sister in Boston, we were called down to CG's immediately. I was worried that the line would get cut if I took the elevator, so I went down the fire escape and walked down the stairs while chatting on the phone. After walking down several sets of stairs, I realized that I had reached the end of the stairwell and was standing in the darkness of a damp basement, surrounded by piping. It was a bit scary so I finally got off the phone to try and find my way back to civilization. I walked all the way back up to our floor and tried to open the door but could not, as the door to the fire escape only opened from the inside. So I walked back down again, and luckily came across a plumber who thankfully led me out of this maze and into the underground parking lot, from where I took the service elevator up to the lobby. That's when it struck me. Every floor had a service elevator which led straight down to the underground parking lot.

I began scheming. I chose a Saturday night to carry out my devious plan, and bribed our very sweet housekeeping lady, Bhakti, to help me out with the added encouragement of a sum of Rs 500 and the promise of getting her at least fifteen recommendations for the employee of the month award. This was the deal: she was going to escort me down the service elevator (which had an access code) and into the parking lot, where Rushab would be awaiting my arrival. She would then meet me back where I had left her, at the door of the elevator, exactly thirty minutes later, to bring me back to the safety of my room. Really, it was pretty simple.

The anticipated day arrived. I was surprised to find myself slightly nervous. On that Saturday evening, I called Rushab. I gave him painfully detailed instructions, my voice dropping to a husky whisper. 'Why can't you do this when I get to the hotel?' Rushab asked. '*Hellooo*, I won't get cellphone reception in that bloody elevator,' I said.

'OK, well speak up 'cuz I am sure there is no need to whisper right now.'

'Umm, yeah. OK,' I said sheepishly as I looked around the Miriam-less room. 'Darling, please just be there on time, OK? You know what a big risk this is.'

'Uh-huh, yeah, yeah, I'll be there on time. No worries,' he replied, his usual confident self. On this end I was freaking out. I really needed to chill. Honestly, what was the worst-case scenario? If anyone ever found out, the *worst* thing that could possibly happen was that I would be kicked out of the pageant. At this point that really didn't seem too awful.

I proceeded with the plan. I wore my sunglasses, darkest clothes and sneakers, to try and seem as inconspicuous as possible. I took the service elevator down, accompanied by Bhakti, and went down into the parking lot, where Rushab's dark-blue Skoda stood, its headlights on high beam. I felt like quite the damsel in distress, led by her loyal maid-in-waiting, escaping the evil castle, to ride away on horseback with her Prince Charming.

'Bhakti, man, you'd better be back here in thirty minutes sharp, there is a big tip in it for you . . . and maybe five more recommendations. I don't want to be stuck here by myself, it's shady.' 'Don't worry ma'am,' replied Bhakti as I squeezed a 500-rupee note into her palm. I opened the car door and dove into Rushab's open arms, but only for a second. I hopped into the back seat and lay down on the floor of the car. 'Riya, dude, what the hell is wrong with you? This Miss Indian Beauty shit has driven you crazy! That floor is dirty, just come sit next to me.' 'Rushab, just drive, okay?' I squeaked from my uncomfortable position on the floor. 'I don't want to be kicked out of this damn pageant.'

'Whatever . . .' He shrugged and stepped on the gas. Seconds later, as we left the hotel, I rose from the dusty floor and fell into his embrace. These were to be the sweetest, most sacred thirty minutes of my life. I took advantage of every second and thoroughly enjoyed my banana split at Baskin Robbins, which I wolfed down in five minutes flat. I didn't even share one bite. The time flew by all too quickly, and before I knew it, I was whisked away from Prince Charming and was back to the confines of the evil castle, or in this case, my room. It had all seemed like a dream, and only the chocolate stains on the front of my shirt were proof of my sins.

Other girls too came up with bold plans to meet their loved ones. Juhi met her boyfriend, a total Lokhandwala boy, complete with fake Diesel jeans, tight t-shirt and black leather boots, in the now-popular underground parking lot. Overcome with desperation, they did not make it quite past that point. What they did in the dark and dank underground parking lot, behind the tinted glasses of his Maruti Esteem, I don't care to imagine.

Others of the group who could not muster up the courage to leave the confines of the hotel found locations within the hotel, from the changing rooms at the poolside to the secluded, under-construction top floor, to an isolated spot on the terrace garden. The power of love takes us all to new extremes, and when Cupid calls, it is impossible to resist.

Back to school

For all of us aspiring beauty queens, aged eighteen and above, it was time to go back to school, but this time sporting stilettos instead of Bata shoes, styled hair instead of oiled plaits, and hip-hugging jeans instead of knee-length skirts. As part of our publicity campaign, we were made to go to schools around the city as advocates of a campaign to promote cleanliness. We donned our Miss Indian Beauty publicity tees, which by this point had become rather soiled, and loaded into our beauty mobile to embark on yet another publicity stunt. This time though, it was slightly more enjoyable, as we were going to schools in the area to interact with the children and talk about ways to keep the environment clean. On the way to the first school, our overexcited publicist, Kajol, who always dressed like she was about to hit the nearest disco, gave us the low-down: 'Remember girls, you are here to promote yourselves and the pageant, remember to mention the sponsors' names whenever possible. Also, remember to use the Fresh! motto of "Feel Fresh!" Remember girls, all the channels will be there, this is your chance to be seen and heard.' Forget about promoting cleanliness, I thought to myself.

We received our first real taste of fame once we arrived at the school. We were welcomed into the school with fanfare as fifteen third-graders puffed away into their horns and banged away at their drums, to no discernable rhythm or tune, perspiring profusely in the heat, dust and humidity of the Mumbai summer. The school's principal welcomed us with garlands of flowers, pasting watery tilaks on our foreheads. The head girl stood beside the principal smiling widely, performing with great care the job consecrated on her by the principal herself, garlanding each and every wannabe beauty queen with attentiveness and concentration.

After this grand welcome, we were split up into groups of threes and fours and assigned to classrooms ranging from kindergarten to second grade, but not before a visit to the bathroom in the principal's office. Here the girls wiped off the saffron tilaks which dotted their foreheads and hurriedly reapplied the make-up which had melted away in the heat and now streaked down their faces from the labour and sweat of climbing up the six flights of stairs, all the while groaning and grumbling about *why* there was no elevator to the principal's office.

After some brisk retouching and a quick SMS or two,

the group proceeded to the various classrooms to give the five-minute sermon on cleanliness, before reassembling on the terrace cafeteria for interviews with the press. We entered the classrooms with cameras on our tail. Certain girls were a bit too enthusiastic, smiling into the lens, 'Our secret to being a Fresh! Miss Indian Beauty is being clean and hygienic, that is what makes us so beautiful, you too can be this beautiful!' Girls clambered and pushed to be part of the limelight, even though they really didn't have much to say. The fact of the matter was this—with less than ten days to go before the pageant, girls were getting more and more desperate for attention, throwing themselves at the camera, doing absolutely anything to be in front of the lens. It was getting worse every day and I could only imagine and fear what would happen on the big night. The girls flirted with the second-grade boys and threw coy smiles at the cameras. I stood awkwardly at the back, feeling once again as if I was back in school, standing at the front of the classroom having been punished by the teacher for bad behaviour.

I heaved a big sigh of relief when we were called up to the terrace for a press meet. On the terrace cafeteria we looked longingly at the golden, freshly-fried samosas oozing with grease, and the dusty bags of chocolates and biscuits, until we were whisked away on to a stage and seated in plastic chairs arranged in rows. At this gathering were present the media, twenty-three sixth-grade girls,

133

and us. On a table in front of us sat twenty-three potted plants, each bearing one of our names. The media then proceeded to ask us questions. 'How do you keep your skin so fair and healthy?' 'By using Fresh! cold cream, of course! We have been giving these girls tips on how to keep their skins fair and glowing like ours . . . and how to keep their surroundings clean.'

The young girls stared at us shyly yet curiously, whispering to each other about who they found the most beautiful. Each contestant then handed a potted plant to each one of the sixth-grade girls, who promised to keep our plant alive and healthy through the long, hot summer.

At last we got up, and I could hear the sighs of relief as girls wiped away the beads of perspiration that were accumulating on their foreheads. The schoolgirls crowded at the foot of the stage, struggling to get a close-up view, pushing each other to be in the front. Two girls smiled at me, and the dusky, slightly plump one nudged the fair, tall girl next to her and shyly said, 'This is Sandya, she is the prettiest girl in the class. She wants to be a model when she grows up.' Another girl piped in, 'She will also be Miss Indian Beauty.' Sandya looked down at the floor, blushing, with a look of pride in her eyes, as some of my contemporaries proudly patted her fair head.

On the way out, as we walked (some of us raced towards the haven of the air-conditioned bus) through the fanfare, a group of children rushed towards us, autograph books in hand, pushing and shoving to get our scribbles in their bright, glossy books.

After repeating the same procedure with pretty much the same response at two other schools, we were ready to go back to the hotel. The entire experience had been pretty hectic and the thought of going back to the cool, serene hotel had never seemed as welcoming as it did on that sweltering afternoon.

We were once again treated to the fare of non-butter, non-cheese, non-everything sandwiches, which were wrapped in plastic. As each one of us dug hungrily into the sandwiches, I was horrified to see several of the plastic wrappers go straight out of the bus windows on to the street outside. Along with the wrappers flew out all the messages of cleanliness we had strived to instill in the children that morning. It was made startlingly clear that afternoon that beauty didn't go beyond hair, make-up and skin.

Disco dhamaka

An outing! That too at a nightclub! I was pumped. Finally, freedom, even if it was for just one night. I was excited at the prospect of having a drink and dancing to good music. The annoying thing was that we weren't told where we were going. It was supposed to be a 'surprise'. Yeah, right. They probably did not want us to call our friends and boyfriends there. I got all jazzed up to go out. I put on make-up, jewellery, the works. We had some pretty high hopes—we were expecting to be rubbing shoulders with the rich and famous, an opulent evening with champagne, caviar, the whole deal . . . OK, this was pushing it, but I at least was expecting a good night out.

We went all dolled up to a shady bar/lounge called 'Tantric'. In all my days of clubbing in Mumbai I had never even heard of this shady place, which was in some obscure corner of Bandra. I was shocked. Granted it was still early, just 10 p.m., but I was expecting at least a few people there. It was totally empty. This really sucked. Even the music was off! As we sulked on the dance floor, the music came on. Sonal came to where a bunch of us were standing and started thrusting to the music, 'Come on girls, dance!' Soon enough, the camera crews came around, and when they did, the girls started dancing wildly to show the world just how much fun the Miss Indian Beauty girls really have.

An hour later, a group of shady teenage boys walked in, sat at the bar and started making eyes at all of us. At this point we were rushed into a private room upstairs. Phew, at least there was a bar here. I went to the bar to get a drink. I needed something strong. 'Could I have a gin and tonic please?'

'Sorry ma'am, only soft drinks. No alcohol.'

'You have *got* to be kidding me!'

'Sorry madam, strict instructions.'

Could this get any worse? Apparently it could. I took the first sip of my Diet Coke. I hadn't had an ounce of caffeine in the past three weeks, and at this rate I could probably get high off a diet coke. Just as I was taking my first sip, Sonal came and snatched the drink away from me. 'Nah-ah! I don't think so! I'll take that from you miss, your drinks are on the table.' I looked across the room to a table where sat several glasses of juice of various colours. Wow, I really had not expected this. The TV crews continued to film us dancing and having oh-so-much fun! So this was

the high point of our 'night out'. In the world of Miss
Indian Beauty, things are never as you expect them to be.

For a beauty queen aspirant, make-up and hair are essential.
It is make-up which transforms her from the girl-next-
door into a beautiful and glamorous beauty queen. It is
make-up which paints on the missing cheekbones, hides
the pimples and stress lines, glues on the missing eyelashes,
and essentially hides all her defects and flaws from the
world. The make-up phenomenon is quite an interesting
one, because make-up does different things for different
people. A very ordinary face can become ravishingly
beautiful with make-up, or it can at times distort the face.
Therefore, we were all curious to witness the effect of
make-up on each other. Which ugly duckling would be
converted into a beauty queen?

On the day of the press conference, we all witnessed
the wonders of make-up when we saw Vasundra, who
surprisingly was the face for Fresh! cold cream despite her
rather inflamed skin, converted from an ordinary pimply
girl into a budding beauty queen. Amisha's plain-Sally face
was painted with colour to transform her into an exotic
beauty. Then there were the others, for whom make-up
didn't really do too much. I was one of these girls. Too bad
it didn't radically change my face; if anything I think heavy

138

make-up made me look worse. The dark eyes and fake eyelashes made my already-tiny eyes look like they had been stung by an insect, and the bright pink blush looked quite gaudy on my small, miniscule face.

The role of a make-up man (or woman) is essential. This is the artist who paints the canvas with vibrant colors to make it come alive, the magician who adds that spark to ignite the fire. Choosing this artist is a task in itself. Throughout the training period we needed make-up people for several different occasions, from the press conference to various fashion shows to the main event. For a make-up artist, being chosen for the Miss Indian Beauty pageant was a pretty big deal, signifying that he or she had come of age in the world of fashion. It was a coveted position, and there was quite a tussle for it.

Prince, our lovely gay make-up man, was the first one in line. He was the first professional make-up person that I had ever had. I will always have fond memories of Prince. He made each one of us feel special, and his mere presence could make any situation a bit brighter. Unfortunately though, everyone had complaints about his work. Lots of girls said that he just wasn't good enough, and that he wasn't doing justice to their faces. Here, in bimboland, rumours spread like wildfire, and once ignited, the Prince-bashing began. Girls blamed Prince for their flawed looks in the portfolios that had been created for us—they blamed him for their missing cheekbones, their thin lips and their nonexistent jaw lines. It went so completely out of control that Yasmeen, who was in charge of choosing the make-up people, caught wind of the situation and finally dismissed poor Prince.

Next came Kapoor, another gay man, but in no way as flamboyant and vibrant as Prince. I can best describe Kapoor in three words—sulky, lumpy and lazy. He didn't really talk much at all, although I tried to initiate a conversation with him several times. I finally resorted to my cellphone. He just sort of sat there, quite dumpy, for most of the time, and would not even bother coming to the set to do our touch-ups. I even caught him snoozing on several occasions, after eating the bag of chips or chocolates that he brought along (which we all eyed with hunger). Despite all of this, everyone seemed to be fairly content with his make-up. That is, until the rumour started that he was unhygienic, and that his make-up had given Juhi three pus-filled pimples. All of a sudden everyone seemed to have broken out with rashes or pimples, and Kapoor was blamed for using his fingers, and for using old foundation and mouldy sponges.

The last one in line was Vimal, who was the only straight guy of the lot. I am quite wary of non-gay male make-up artists, as I have noticed that often the best and most popular professionals in this business are mostly gay men. I fail to understand why there aren't enough good women in this profession in India. Vimal had the reputation of being one of the best and most experienced professionals in the industry, and as I had expected, soon the gushing started about how Vimal's make-up was perfect, and how he was just right for the event. Vimal just didn't have the same panache and flair that Prince did. Unfortunately, Vimal wasn't available for the night of the big event, so we had to make do with the lumpy Kapoor. I should not comment as I have not had too much experience in this area, but honestly I did not see the big difference between Prince's and Kapoor's work. I missed Prince, with his puckish eyes and mischievous smile, and I have to admit, I still have the biggest crush on him.

Our first taste of the diamonds

It's a big myth that models have it easy. They don't, and I was to discover this rather painfully. Traditionally, exactly one week before the big night, the crowns that are to be presented to the winners are unveiled to the public. Apparently, this was the first time in the history of beauty pageants around the world that real diamond crowns were being presented to the winners. In the past, materials used for the crowns ranged from glass to American diamonds to Swarovski crystals, but never the real thing.

For the unveiling of the crowns we were to put on a small fashion show, wearing outfits in the sponsor colours of turquoise and white, along with some rather spectacular diamond jewellery. With the finale just a week away, Yasmeen thought it well advised to add some complex choreography to the event, rather than simply having us walk out contestant-number-wise, as we had earlier done for the press conference.

It was then that I realized how truly complicated all of this was. Honestly, to walk down that ramp in uncomfortable shoes, with a smile plastered on your face, remembering music cues for entry, and all the twisting and turning that goes on on that ramp, is quite difficult. To add to all these woes, choreographers aren't really the sweetest or easiest people to work with. I heard from some of the other girls that Yasmeen was one of the nicest choreographers out there. At this point, Yasmeen had become quite the devil, and I really could not imagine how choreographers could get worse than this. Apparently other choreographers would add to the screaming by kicking, and sometimes even resort to a smack or two when things didn't go right.

We practiced in CG's on a make-believe ramp created with chairs. Yasmeen must have been PMSing or something, because I had never seen her this evil. She even brought a few of the more sensitive girls to tears. Under her careful eye we walked down our makeshift stage, smiles plastered on to our faces as we shivered with fear on the inside. I have never had a good sense of direction, so I was just miserable at all of this. It just seemed terribly hard to multitask—remembering the walk, the smile, the music, the directions. And I had thought I was a great multitasker

143

because I was double majoring in college!

After what seemed like hundreds of hours of practice, our feet swollen and bruised, Yasmeen deemed the presentation acceptable. Now that we had the choreography under control, the next step was the fittings. Fittings are always quite nerve-wracking, and particularly so when it comes to beauty pageants, where there is stiff competition. It was during these fitting sessions that the outfits for the show were handed out, usually at random. We crossed our fingers and fervently hoped to get an outfit that we fancied, one that did justice to our figure and of a colour that complimented our skin tone. It was always amusing to see faces either fall or light up with joy when outfits were first handed off the rack, into the eagerly waiting arms of the contestant. Sometimes, if one was lucky, outfits could be changed, but that was a rare occurrence. In most cases you were stuck with whatever you were handed out that first time. There was a handful of girls who always had problems with the way their outfits looked and would complain to no end about it. These were generally the 'no rice-roti' girls, who were made so self-conscious about their bodies that they developed a deep insecurity about the way they looked.

For the unveiling of the crowns, we were given gowns in white and different shades of blue. Some of these gowns were rather racy, with sheer tops or side slits that went right up to the hips, and some with necklines that plunged disturbingly low. To find appropriate undergarments for these outfits was quite a mission. Many of us went door-to-door on our floor, begging to borrow an appropriate bra, and in some desperate cases, even some form of panties. Despite this, several of us just could not piece together the correct underwear, and many of us had panty lines showing through the figure-hugging bottoms, which looked quite vulgar. Yasmeen was quite exasperated and she gave each of us a 'stick-on bra' and a pair of pantyhose.

The stick-on bra/nude bra is truly a blessing to all womankind, and for the modelling industry it is most definitely *the* invention of the twenty-first century. After having been oblivious to its existence all these years, it had quite an impact on me. Imagine, no more bra problems for the rest of my life! The ingenious product that I write of basically consists of silicon cups which look and feel like the real thing, and sticks on to your breasts. Never again would I have to worry about straps or sagging bras. To deal with the other half of the problem we had pantyhose with the legs cut off, which actually work really well as seamless underwear. With our stick-on bras and pantyhose we were ready to face the public.

On the day of the unveiling, we woke up early in the morning, at 5 a.m., to begin the make-up process, which usually took about six hours for all of us. Once this long process was over, we piled into our beauty mobile, undergarments in tow, and headed for the venue. On arrival we hastily changed into our outfits and practiced a few times on stage with a rather frazzled Yasmeen. Things were a lot easier now that we had an actual ramp, and not just chairs marking the area. After a few practice runs we all went backstage into the 'green room'. 'Green room' was the new word that I had learned through this pageant. I have absolutely no clue why it is called a green room, but this is the name given to the make-up room backstage where touch-ups are done. The arrival of the jewellery which we were to wear for the show led to a situation of extreme chaos and subsequent disaster, as girls rushed towards the overwhelmed staff. The idea was this—if you're the last to be bejewelled you will be handed out the 'worst' jewellery, which in this case meant a smaller necklace or lighter earrings. This was a complete misconception, because much like our outfits, all the jewellery was of approximately the same value and size, and was handed out at random. In the mad rush for the diamonds, I heard several rips, followed by wails of anguish. After the catastrophic and unruly behavior which was displayed that evening, jewellery was always handed out contestant-number-wise.

As we waited backstage we were told that we could each have two guests for the show. I guessed we were informed about this at the last minute because they were probably unable to gather a big enough crowd for the event. This led to a wave of excitement among the girls, and cellphones were immediately whipped out. I called up Rushab and Shreeya to invite them to the event, eager to have them critique my walk down the ramp and also see each one of my competitors in close proximity.

After a long wait backstage, where the girls spent much of their time flirting with the members of the band which was performing for the occasion, we were summoned to take our place behind the curtains. The long wait had jaded me, and I just wanted the show to be over. I didn't feel the slightest tingle of nervousness or excitement. I just wanted to get out of my painful shoes, get all the pins out of my hair, and go see Rushab.

I waited to hear my music cue. It's always a strange feeling to walk down the ramp for real after so many practice runs. The blinding lights, the crowd, the raging applause—it's all so different, and gets over in a flash. My turn finally arrived, and as I took the ramp I scanned the crowd for Rushab and found him sitting alone on one side, wearing a rather amused look, clearly entertained by this entire display.

The show that we had rehearsed for hours lasted exactly five minutes and twenty-four seconds. Five minutes and twenty-four seconds to show for all our hard work. After my two seconds of glory, we all re-emerged as a group and assembled on the stage, standing motionless, smiles fixed on to our painted faces. This had to be the most torturous experience that I have ever been through. I stood there balancing myself on my swollen feet, immobile, smiling until the sides of my face ached, while the press took picture after picture. Corny fanfare music along with the cheesy Star Wars tune came on, and the three crowns were brought up on a hydraulic lift along with smoke and glitter. All this while I could only concentrate on the extreme pain and anguish that I was going through, till finally everything became numb and I could feel no more. After a million photographs and what seemed like an eternity, we were done. I cannot even begin to explain what a relief it was.

I was excited that Rushab was coming. Even though he had been coming to see me religiously on Sundays, this was his first public appearance, for all eyes to feast on. I was bursting with excitement to see him, and so were the other contestants, especially Preeti, who was perhaps the strangest of all of us, and it would not be an understatement to say that we had some pretty strange girls there. Preeti was one of our army girls. She was an engineering student who had been modelling for the past year or so after being one of the finalists at the Metropolitan Model Hunt. She was dedicated to winning the crown, and would have done close to anything to have it. She had been scouring every single general knowledge book she could get her hands on, and had begun a career in modelling only to prepare for the Miss Indian Beauty pageant. She had given it all that she could, and was now ready to win.

Preeti had a curious personality, with an air of mystery surrounding her, which could very well have been assumed. I never really understood Preeti, and neither did anyone else for that matter. At times I felt she was treading the fine line between sanity and psychoticness. I would not have been surprised to see her break tables and chairs if she didn't win that crown—she wanted it that badly. Like her personality, her face was rather curious. I could not make up my mind if she was really pretty, or really ugly. She had a wide-set face, with small eyes that lent her an 'eastern' look. She had one of those faces that some could find exceptionally exotic, whereas others could find extremely disproportionate. I always admired Preeti's body, though it could have done with some toning. She was on the taller side, with a willowy, graceful frame. Preeti had gone all-out to prepare a wardrobe for this contest, arriving with tagged outfits paired with matching shoes and bags meant for each day of the week. I never really did understand her sense of style, though one could see that she had put in a lot of effort to assemble an entire wardrobe, jewellery, shoes and bags included. She would wear some outfits which were in good taste on certain days, but on other days she would wear extremely flashy and gaudy outfits of the 'Indo-Western' look, with embroidered cholis in garish colours coupled with contrasting long, flowy skirts. She had the body to flaunt, and so she did just that. She would wear the skimpiest of clothing, and she got away with it rather well.

Could she win the crown? I thought so—she had the body, the speech, the exotic looks, and even though I suspected she had some serious mental issues, she disguised them rather well.

Preeti had been inquiring about Rushab, and going on and on about how she wanted to meet him ever since the day I told her I had a boyfriend. Why would *they* care to see *my* boyfriend? There was a very simple and rather logical reason for this. You see, there was constant judging going on among the contestants. Someone or the other was always watching and scrutinizing your every move and action, judging, trying to figure out who you really were, trying to see what lay under all the make-up. What better way to judge someone than through her boyfriend? In most species of animals, the 'healthiest' female will claim the strongest or most attractive mate, so the attractiveness of my mate would reflect on my 'health', and all the girls, like animals in the wild, were trying to judge how 'healthy' I was. Some people took it to new extremes. Rushab and I sat down in the separate enclosure that had been created for the contestants and their guests to make sure we didn't mingle with the crowd. I strategically chose two seats in the middle of the row, as people tend to occupy the borders and wouldn't make the effort of centralizing themselves. As we took our places, Preeti, being her slightly psychotic self, came and chose a seat right behind us, placing herself on the very edge of her chair, eavesdropping on every word that passed between us. To make it worse, when I went to refill my plate, she went ahead and initiated a conversation with Rushab! After this experience, I dragged Rushab to a corner and made sure he was safe from prying eyes. It really was quite a jungle out there.

It wasn't too long before we had to go for another photo shoot. This was the first time that I would see the crowns up close and personal. They took my breath away. The crowns were beautiful, cast with glittering diamonds, rubies, sapphires and gold. Each crown represented one of the elements, the first crown fire, the second water, and the third earth. The three crowns rested on their velvet thrones, encased in glass, just out of our reach. We all stared at them, the diamonds reflecting in our eyes and the desire burning in our hearts.

After reluctantly tearing our eyes off the resplendent crowns, we all assembled for a photo with the seventeen-year-old son of the CEO of the sponsor. He looked thrilled as girls grabbed on to his arms, not because he was even remotely attractive, but because they wanted to be the focal point of the picture. They batted their fake eyelashes at him and enthralled him with seductive smiles. I could see his thrill gradually transform into nervousness as the girls grew increasingly aggressive with the flash of the cameras.

After the photo shoot I rushed backstage, kicked off my killer heels, put on my sneakers and struggled to get all the pins out of my hair, as I had now developed a splitting headache. Following this, I spent some time with Rushab, trying to keep him away from prying eyes.

At last, we were done. It was close to midnight, and all I wanted to do was to remove all my make-up, take a steaming hot shower, change into my favorite pyjamas (the ones with the hole in the backside), and snuggle into bed.

On the way back I was lost in thought. There was something different in the way I felt during that initial press conference and this event. I couldn't pinpoint it, but this time around there was something missing. Even though this was only the second time that I had walked down the ramp, it had seemed like a spent experience. That spark of novelty which I had felt during my first catwalk had been extinguished. That flame had died in such a short period of time, and maybe that is one of the reasons why I never got a taste of those diamonds.

The beauty bible

Just about a week before the contest, all was forgotten—
the catwalk, the daily fashion parade, the fatigue—and the
girls were hit by a new storm. At this point in the training
program, we all realized that our looks, height and bodies
could only get us so far. The factor that would finally clinch
the crown would be the Q&A round. The Miss Indian
Beauty pageant has two question rounds. The first would
consist of the ten semi-finalists, chosen on the day of the
pre-judging. In this round, each girl would be asked to
pick the name of a judge, who would then pose a question
to the contestant. This process was to be repeated ten times,
with nine judges questioning nine girls, and the last question
was to be asked by the winner of the Coffee Bean Cafe
contest. Following this, five finalists were to be selected,
and this time there would be one common question for all
five girls. The answers to this question would be penned

down by each girl in the span of a minute, after which she would read out her answer. From these five, based on the answers to the common question, the three winners would be selected. After the pre-judging, the ability to answer questions well was all that mattered. At the beginning of the training period, we had each been given a book which held a bank of about a hundred and fifty beauty pageant questions. Sonal had told us that it would be in our best interests to 'mug up' all these questions. The book also contained a list of quotes. I hadn't seen these books for the past twenty days, but now each girl clutched the book close to her heart. The same book that was once tossed into a corner of the room underneath a pile of clothes, shoes and hair products, now re-emerged and was carried in every purse with reverence. It was given almost the same level of importance as the prized lip-gloss or hairbrush. Other than this 'beauty bible', newspapers were in great vogue, as the girls figured they must be 'aware' of what was going on outside our bubble world. Several girls had brought along various varieties of 'question banks', among which a popular one was a book of beauty pageant questions compiled by Malvika Kapoor, a VJ and aspiring actress who I don't think ever even ran for a beauty pageant.

By this time, I had got the gist of answering these rather frivolous beauty pageant questions quite well. It was actually pretty simple. There are only so many topics on which questions can be posed, some of the more popular ones include beauty, values (honesty, morality, humility etc.), current affairs, women (the essence of being a woman and all that). Once the major topics are known, it's not difficult to spout a similar answer for all of them. The second task is creating a list of favourites—favourite author, favourite food, favourite book, favourite person. Hopefully, you have a reason behind each answer, and voila, you're pretty much prepared for the beauty pageant. By practicing these two things I had established myself as the undisputed Q&A queen, and several of the girls would come to me asking for help, which I would gladly give in return for a catwalk session or two. This position had its drawbacks as well. Every time I would open a book or a newspaper, or even sit down to write my journal, either Amisha or Prachi (or both), perhaps the most intense of the girls, would come snooping around to see what I was doing, to the point that they would see what article I was reading in the newspaper, hunt out the same one, and begin to read it. As things got more intense, several girls found their treasured books missing, which was a bit difficult to understand because each one of us had been given the same book. I thought this was all D-Day drama, until the same thing happened to me.

As the big day drew closer and closer, the frenzy reached a whole new level. It came to the point that Q&A was all that was talked about. Amazingly, all the talk of clothes, bags, boyfriends and society gossip came to a standstill.

This was really the first time that I came across semi-constructive conversations, as girls attempted to discuss politics, books and 'current affairs'. Though the Q&A frenzy was enormously hyped, I do believe that it may have got static minds ticking, and some girls discovered the cerebral in themselves for perhaps the very first time.

Curiosity killed the cat

Throughout the training period, girls scrutinized the competition intensely. Comparatively, through the course of twenty-five days, this level of intensity had significantly reduced towards the middle part. As the day of the contest edged closer, there was a revival of the intensity with which this analysis was carried out. The girls spent their time doing one of two things—either stressing over Q&A, or stressing over their competition, both of which were bound to have detrimental effects. The level of analysis reached new levels as girls closely examined each other from head to toe, hair and skin, and drew their own conclusions as to who was competition for sub-contest titles. They examined each other on Q&A capabilities, stage presence, beauty, body and skin. Lists were constructed on the expected top ten, and then compared and discussed with fervour. Some girls even went ahead and performed a seance, attempting to call on spirits to reveal the winner, perhaps hoping that these spirits would reveal questions that they themselves would be asked.

I became completely antisocial, keeping to myself, trying to escape the negative energy that was being projected in all directions. I realized that this contest was of paramount importance to many of these girls. They had devoted days, months, years, and countless sleepless nights to be here, but all this crazy scrutiny and aggressive competition was creating a bad vibe. This negative competition could only result in one of two things—over-confidence or over-anxiety. The one and perhaps only useful thing that I had learnt through Donald's sessions was that you had to compete only with yourself. You had to break through both mental and physical barriers to bring out the best in yourself. There was nothing to be gained by competing against each other. Nothing, except for negativity, hostility and malice, which would only drain our energy levels.

A few days before the pre-judging round, Mr Parek started coming in for brief 'Q&A' sessions, though they were more like pseudo-inspirational talks. These, not surprisingly, failed to inspire us, and just lead to more nervousness. He would discuss a few topics, pose a few irrelevant questions, and bounce out of there. He would leave feeling quite important, as in desperation many girls were becoming increasingly servile, and some were even going as far as casting seductive looks in his direction. The first time that he came, he gave a rather a bogus inspirational speech in which I think he was trying to warn us to a certain extent. I remember his words clearly: 'Don't talk too much, don't think you're smarter than anyone else, and don't try to demotivate others, because it'll only lead to your end.' I don't know why he did this, but it was probably to prevent last minute mishaps.

Our final session with Mr Parek was strange. He wanted to meet each of us individually for 'personal counselling', to 'help each one of us out with our individual problems'. I was the last person to be called upon. When I went in, Sonal pulled out my file (I wonder what *that* held) and handed it to him. He glanced at it for a while, and then proceeded to make some notes on a piece of paper that lay before him. 'Riya, Riya, Riya . . . what do you think is your biggest drawback?' I thought for a second. There was the fact that I could not walk straight in heels, but that seemed like a somewhat trivial answer. I wanted to give him something deeper than that. I replied, 'You know, Mr Parek, till date, with less than a week to go before the big day, I have still not digested the fact that I am a part of this. I can't believe that I am here. This is probably my biggest drawback.' He looked slightly bewildered at my answer. He blinked his beady eyes behind the tortoise-shell glasses, and rubbed his hands together as he was in the habit of doing. He stared at me, and I twitched in discomfort. 'Riya, if there was one thing that you could change about the training period what would it be?' I took a minute to think. 'I live by my organizer, and haphazard planning bothers me to a certain extent, because I am not a spontaneous person, really. If we could find a way to make this pageant better organized . . .' All the while that I spoke, he took notes on the piece of paper in front of him. I got up to leave, and he followed me out. As I reached for the door, he touched my shoulder. I turned around. 'Riya, I think you are a high-potential candidate.' I smiled, and it wasn't one of my practiced smiles.

Everyone's 'counselling' had been similar to mine. He hadn't really counselled us; rather, he had analyzed each one of us. I overheard girls saying they had reached a state of tears while talking to him, not out of fear or sadness, but because of the emotion he had invoked in them. Others said that he knew all sorts of quirky details—how someone dressed, or with whom they had established particularly strong friendships. He had been watching us through the eyes of the chaperones who were always with us, very, very closely. But why? Why should he care at all? After all, he was only in charge of organizing the pageant. Of what advantage was this analysis to him? I couldn't figure it out. It was then that I started wondering, really wondering what was going on behind the scenes of this beauty pageant.

Throughout the course of our one-month training session, we had guest speakers come and speak to us. These speakers generally hailed from the media industry. As most girls wanted to pursue a career in the media world, only people from showbiz could hold the attention of the entire group. Even though these sessions would often take place at the end of a long, gruelling day, and I would grumble at having to attend them, I learnt to appreciate them for what they were. Each speaker had a story to tell, and within each story there was meaning and a moral. These lessons were important. This contest would thrust three girls into the world of glamour, which can be a difficult world to tackle. These individuals told us of their personal experiences, battles, failures and successes in the industry, and threw light on the peculiar world of showbiz.

When we were told that we were to have an ex-Miss Indian Beauty of substantial fame speak to us, we were all quite excited. Who could it possibly be? Of course, we were all hoping it would be one of the international crown winners who had then consequently had Bollywood fame, someone along the lines of Tara Dutt or Priya Chopra, or if we got really lucky, Alisha Ray or Meeta Sengupta. These individuals were probably too busy to address a bunch of wannabe Miss Indian Beauties, so we had to make do with Gulpreet Narula, who, after losing at the Miss Universal

Beauty pageant had disappeared into post-Miss Indian Beauty oblivion. She had re-emerged into the limelight now that she was entering the movies. It was amazing how well set the Bollywood track was for Miss Indian Beauty participants. After winning the pageant, and after immediately fulfilling the year-long duties of a Miss Indian Beauty, the winners almost immediately headed for Bollywood. I could not think of any Miss Indian Beauty who had done it differently.

This was the first time that we were to talk to someone who had successfully participated in the Miss Indian Beauty pageant. After Mamta Sindhu's return from the Miss Universal Beauty pageant in the early '90s, where she had lost narrowly, the Miss Indian Beauty training program that had begun on a fairly modest scale had reached the level of lavishness at which it stood today. This year we were quite lucky to have the Grand Hotel as our sponsor, who had put us up in their five-star facilities. The year that Gulpreet Narula ran, the girls had to find their own accommodation and commute every morning to their modest training facilities. The Miss Indian Beauty pageant had come a long way, from training sessions held in non-air-conditioned school classrooms to the comfort of a five-star hotel.

Gulpreet's story was quite an inspiring one, of how she rose to instant fame with her crowning, from a humble defence background. She led us through the journey of her experience as a young, immature girl who won the

Miss Indian Beauty pageant, of her experience in the international arena and why she failed, of her life afterwards, and now, her entry into the world of cinema. I could relate very well to Gulpreet, who spoke of her initial nervousness at competing with top models, but then rising above the apprehension and emerging as the winner. The most interesting part of her talk was her look into the Miss Universal Beauty pageant and the factors, according to her, which had led to her defeat. She told us that at the pageant she was one of the more well-spoken of the bunch as compared to some of the others, many of whom did not have a very good grasp of the English language. For her, the biggest drawback was her physique. The three rounds that led to a place in the top ten of the pageant were the Q&A round, the evening gown round and the swimsuit round. All the contestants received close to equal marking for the evening gown round. Gulpreet had received one of the higher scores in the Q&A round, but it was in the swimsuit round where Gulpreet said she had lagged behind.

So what was it that recent Miss Indian Beauties were lacking? Why was it that we were not able to clinch the international crown for over five years? Gulpreet believed that the girl representing India at the Miss Universal Beauty pageant had to be truly cosmopolitan in every sense of the word, from the way she spoke to the way she dressed, and the way she carried herself, and most importantly, in the way she thought. This is what the recent Miss Indian

Beauties had been lacking, and this is what had led to the recent failures.

Gulpreet's story encouraged me. By this point, even though I was naturally inclined towards overconfidence, I was starting to feel nervous. I was trying pretty hard, but I just couldn't seem to get it right. I was going to CG's night after night and practicing on the ramp. My feet had never been in worse shape, and I was in dire need of a pedicure. I was struggling with myself to become a part of this, and release myself from the fear of people finding out about my taking part. There was no reason why I would not be able to do it, I thought to myself. Some of Donald's wistful mumbo-jumbo was starting to rub off on me. I had to have faith in the future. If it was meant to happen, it would. Faith was honestly the only thing I had going for me at that moment.

The fate of a Miss Indian Beauty

It is interesting to look at the annals of the Miss Indian Beauty pageant and examine its evolution over the past twenty years. What have past Miss Indian Beauties done with their lives? Where do they stand today? How has this pageant changed? We had the chance to find out when Sadhna Swaroop came as a guest speaker. Sadhna Swaroop was crowned Miss Indian Beauty in the '70s, after which she took her first trip abroad to attend the Miss Universal Beauty pageant held in Los Angeles. She received no training, had to design all her own clothes, and even had to pay her own airfare. She wore a swimsuit for the first time in her life at the pageant. For the evening gown round she wore a gold zari sari with a matching choli. She coupled this outfit with ornate gold jewellery and included a 'maang tikka', which was the hit of the evening. She won the best evening gown award. These were the nascent years of the pageant, a time when for a pretty, ambitious Indian girl, perhaps the only cemented path to stardom was to become a Miss Indian Beauty. In Indian society twenty years ago, it was unheard of for a girl from a respectable household to move to Mumbai to pursue her Bollywood dreams. With Westernization and liberalization, all this began to change. It's fairly commonplace now for a middle-class girl to pack her bags and move to Mumbai for a few years to seek Bollywood fame. With the advent of reality TV shows, multiple paths towards stardom opened up as each channel launched 'talent searches' of their own. From 'Look Luscious' on TV-One to 'Metropolitan Model Hunt' to 'Indian Diva', numerous opportunities became available. The Miss Indian Beauty pageant, which was the forerunner in the race, years ahead of the game, became just another player.

The list of girls who rose to fame and fortune due to this pageant goes on and on. It includes Perle Khanna, the Miss Indian Beauty of the '60s who even made a mark in Hollywood, Ruhi Dutta, Neeta Shirode, Priya Batra (runners-up), Meeta Sengupta, Alisha Ray, Tara Dutt and Priya Chopra among so many others. The Miss Indian Beauty contest, first held in 1947, went through colossal change. The first big step towards improvement was the initiation of the training program, which started off as a one-week crash course held in school classrooms, to where it stands today, a one-month intensive training program held in five-star facilities. The Miss Indian Beauty pageant received a reinvigorating boost in the early '90s, when two out of the three winners brought home international crowns. The hype went into overdrive as India proclaimed its arrival on the 'world beauty map', a producer of 'global beauties'. All the miracles of science, from sparkling teeth to beautiful bosoms, were made available to the three winners of the Miss Indian Beauty pageant, and securing these international titles suddenly became a prestige issue.

Eventually, similar to what happened in the West, as with the rage behind the once-hugely popular Miss UK and Miss America pageants in the '80s, the Miss Indian Beauty pageant too slowly came to settle at a mere a fizzle. As the international crowns increasingly evaded Indian crests, the Miss Indian Beauty pageant too began fading away into the dust, leaving behind only a faint trace in Bollywood.

I was excited when I heard that the legendary genius, the notorious Mr Promod Kakre, India's mad 'ad-man', was to come and speak to us. Mr Kakre owned one of India's largest and most successful advertising agencies, and had established a rather infamous reputation on the Page 3 columns. I was quite surprised when I heard that this man, with his self-confessed fetish for beautiful young things, was even allowed to come address the Miss Indian Beauty girls.

Mr Kakre was exactly as I had imagined him to be, clad in his loose Buddha pants teamed with a crumpled linen shirt, and a cowboy hat which was his trademark. His beady eyes twinkled in his dark, wrinkled face, which was covered by shaggy white whiskers and a beard that desperately needed to be trimmed.

I have a feeling he came to 'check out' the girls, to see if any of them were good enough to put in an ad. He was always on the lookout for pretty girls—it was his job. He came in and began chattering away immediately, but most of it really did not make too much sense, I thought. He was rather vague, and obviously had not thought the occasion important enough to prepare for. I was close to falling asleep, when suddenly I was jolted back to attention. Mr Kakre asked us to raise our hand if we wanted to enter the media industry. Everyone in the room raised their hand except for me. I was a bit offended, as he was obviously hinting from the various comments that he was making, that one entered Miss Indian Beauty only to enter the world of the media. I begged to differ. 'Excuse me, Mr Kakre?' He looked surprised.

'Yes?'

'I beg to differ. I don't think that Miss Indian Beauty is a contest held just to enter the movies. The pageant aims to find a girl who epitomizes India in every way, from her beauty to her morals to her intelligence. She is the paragon of Indian womanhood, and has the responsibility of representing the Indian woman at a global level.' God, I sounded like I had stepped straight out of the beauty bible. I must have sounded staggeringly corny.

'OK, well then . . . Miss . . .'

'Riya.'

'Nice name, Riya. Unique. Ok then, *Riya,* why don't you name for me a single Miss Indian Beauty who has done anything other than join the movies to rise to stardom. Can you name a Miss Indian Beauty who has gone on to become an acclaimed academic or activist?'

'Well, I am not saying that, but entering the movies is not the point of this pageant, that's all I want to say.'

He laughed loudly, raising his head up high. A bit of his moustache went into his mouth. 'Listen, babe.'

'Please don't call me babe, Mr Kakre.' I was getting angry now.

'*Wah, wah*, we have quite a chingari here! Listen Riya, if you weren't pretty, and you are quite pretty, you wouldn't be here: the Miss Indian Beauty title is only a certification of your beauty. It is a stamp of approval that you are beautiful enough to be in the movies, and once you are branded, the signal turns green and you are allowed to go.'

I had no reply to give him. I thought I might as well shut up. I was obviously pathetically failing to support my argument.

That was the end of the session. It had lasted only twenty minutes, but it made me think for hours afterwards. My argument with Mr Kakre had unleashed the thoughts that I had pushed away into a corner of my mind. They had now emerged again with a vengeance. I wasn't here to make it in the movies, so why was I here? What did I want out of this? Like everyone else, I wanted fame and glory, but was being Miss Indian Beauty going to get me that?

I had always wondered about the fate of the Miss Indian Beauty girls who didn't win the crown. Did being a part of the pageant help them out in their Bollywood careers, or would it be an indefinite source of embarrassment, like I figured it would be for me . . . if I lost.

It was interesting to have Maya Doshi come and speak to us, as she had run for the Miss Indian Beauty pageant the year that Gulpreet Narula had won. She had been very close to winning the coveted crown, losing by a whisker after she had made it to the top five. Four years later, Maya had finally made her Bollywood debut, and even though the film was a flop, her performance had been critically acclaimed and had marked her place in the world of cinema.

After a full day of activity, it had seemed that Maya's

lecture would be of no consequence, and most of the girls didn't really want to listen to the ramblings of someone who hadn't even won the crown. When I think about it now, we got quite a bit out of it. It was reassuring. It gave confidence to the girls who had waited all their lives for this moment: *if* they didn't win that crown, they would be okay, and though it might seem like the end of the world, it really wasn't. Maya Doshi had done well for herself. Even after losing, she had fought her way through, treaded the stormy sea of Bollywood, and had now finally arrived.

Maya told us that she had lost because she had never practiced writing down answers. If you make it to the top five, you have to pen down an answer full of fluff and fuzz in the span of one minute. Since she had never practiced this, she had lost her nerve at the final instant, and was unable to pen down an appropriate answer. The next day I saw that all the girls were equipped with paper, pens and stopwatches, frantically scribbling away answers to questions from the beauty bible.

After Maya's talk, I realized that there is actually a well-established sequence at play here. First you become a ramp model, which is fairly simple with all the international modelling agencies now coming to India (as long as you meet the 5'6" cut-off and have a decent face). Ramp modelling is a rather lucrative business, paying about Rs 8000 on average for each show, assuring a decent lifestyle through the initial struggles. After achieving some amount of success in this field, the next step is the ad world. This nut is more difficult to crack, and entails going from office to office with a portfolio, desperately hoping that someone will like you enough to sign you 'on contract', which basically means you become the brand ambassador for a product, which could be anything from tea bags to shampoo to air-conditioners. This step is often coupled with another, more recent and popular phenomenon—music-video mania. Rather than a TV serial, a provocative, and if you are lucky, controversial, music video is often a quick and sure-shot way to get noticed. It also prepares you to 'get comfortable' in front of the camera—whatever that means. I have a feeling it might be a hint at the 'bare all' reputation that music videos have achieved these days. The next and final step is the movies, which are the ultimate goal.

The Miss Indian Beauty crown is an assured short cut to the final goal. Every girl starts out as a ramp model, and very slowly makes her way to the top. All this while she keeps her fingers tightly crossed, hoping that she has the stamina to stay in the race, and prays that someone better doesn't come along and overtake her.

The making of a Miss Indian Beauty

What goes behind the making of a beauty queen? From our hair, to our skin and our table manners, we were 'groomed' to perfection. Along with the three trainers that we met every day, Yasmeen, Donald and Emma, we had an entire team of 'experts' who we saw on a regular basis throughout that month. Apparently, we had the 'best of the best' at out disposal for the 'development of every aspect of our personality', as Mr Parek put it. So why would these busy people waste their time on a bunch of Miss Indian Beauty girls? I realized why when I opened the newspaper. Every day throughout that month, our 'expert trainers' would be publicized. Columns praised and applauded their techniques and all the great 'work' they did on us. So, did we benefit from our team of experts? Well, you can decide for yourself.

The smile is of utmost importance to an aspiring beauty queen. It holds almost as much importance as a good pair of legs. It is through that smile that she portrays her confidence, grace and charm. It is through that smile that she seduces and captivates the judges and the audience. It is that smile which has to remain plastered on her face throughout the pageant, not leaving her visage for a single second. It is that smile which conceals the nervousness, the anxiety, and the great discomfort caused by a painful pair of heels. We are all born knowing how to smile. Like love or sex, it is a human instinct.

According to Dr Sandesh Shetty, we are not born knowing how to smile in the *right* way, and that is the job of a 'smile doctor'. Dr Shetty taught us the 'beauty queen' smile, taking us through the various stages of a smile, to be used during the different stages of a beauty pageant. The quarter-smile for all occasions, the half-smile for when we were close to the camera, the three-quarter smile for when we were in focus, and the full smile for our moment of victory. That is what we learnt from Dr Shetty—how to enchant the audience with our carefully practiced smiles, which perfectly concealed the whirlwind of emotions that lay within each one of us. Oh yes—in addition to teaching us how to smile, he taught us the exacting art of brushing and flossing our teeth as well.

Another day, early in the morning, we were dragged out of our comfortable beds at 6 a.m. to be taught the rules that every proper young lady was meant to follow, particularly if you were a proper young lady aspiring to be a beauty queen. We were brought down to listen to the ramblings of Mona Mitthal, who was currently very popular with Page 3. She was clad in a white linen suit, and carried a Louis Vuitton bag daintily in her perfectly manicured hands. I could smell the stale odour of last night's indulgences on her, which wasn't too well disguised by her French perfume. I had no clue why these Page 3 figures claimed to be etiquette gurus.

I became aware of some very important things that morning. Things like how one should shower three times a day, and that too with cold water, how to walk, sit, and lay down like a lady, how to bathe in the correct fashion (with special emphasis on which parts of the body we must not neglect), what a lady must carry in her purse, and other such seemingly apparent things that I am sure each one of us already knew. (Or at least I hope so!) Other than the obvious stuff she told us some rather curious bits and pieces of information, such as the three places to spray perfume: close to your collar bone, on your wrist, and most interestingly, in between your legs. I guess that bit may have come from personal experience.

The other session that we were all very eager to attend was our 'dining etiquette' class with Lina Hussain. It's not that we were overexcited about learning the table manners which most of us hopefully already knew, but because the session was to be accompanied by a seven-course meal. No more diet food—we were to be served chicken, cheese, dessert, the works. We were all excited at the prospect of indulgence after the past three weeks of austerity. Lina Hussain was another Page 3 personality, who after a stint as an air hostess had married a steel tycoon (who she met on first class), and had now opened an 'etiquette school'.

Lina Hussain had no idea what was in store for her that evening. What she assumed would be a group of graceful, composed, lady-like Miss Indian Beauty aspirants, in actuality turned out to be a group of ravenous, carb-starved, meat-crazy, stressed-out girls. All instructions were ignored as the focal point of the session became the grilled chicken that was to be served as the main course. The chiming of the cutlery was used to attract the attention of the servers. The few drops of the mediocre wine that we were served created a sensation amongst the group, as the girls begged and pleaded to be served more. The climax of the evening was when Shanaz was deprived of her non-vegetarian entrée, as it had run out. She had a fit, and at the end of it was close to tears. She had to be compensated with an extra plate of dessert. There was chaos that evening as Lina struggled to get us to pay attention to the glasses, forks and knives. Juhi, who considered herself to be an authority on the subject, as she had been a stewardess for five years, switched on her loudspeaker to let us know that she knew the ins and outs of fine dining. Poor Lina had not expected any of this, and the soft-spoken, cultured lady finally gave up her attempts to exercise control over this rowdy bunch. By the end of the meal our stomachs were happy, even though we all suffered the unfortunate consequences of our gluttony the next morning. What can I say—no pain, no gain. After that wild evening, Lina Hussain vowed never again to return for an etiquette lesson with the ravenous Miss Indian Beauty girls.

Every profession has its drawbacks. For an investment banker it is the long hours, for an athlete it is injury to the joints, and for a model/actor, or in this case an aspiring beauty queen, it is the hair and skin that suffer the maximum damage due to the continuous styling and make-up. By the end of that one month, my hair and skin were in a disastrous state, and we were all in dire need of professional help. Thus we had the 'only trichologist in India' (scientific name for hair doctor) come to our aid. We each got something which resembled a sonogram done to our scalps and were quite taken aback to see our scalps and hair up close and personal. The 'treatment' which we received did not really do much. Each of us were prescribed vitamin pills and given a complimentary bottle of oil, which we were advised to apply daily. For the next few days, several girls sported a rather greasy look in an attempt to recover the health of their tresses before the 'Miss Heavenly Hair' sub-contest.

Next we met our dermatologist, Dr Malika Kapoor. She came in to help us recover our 'natural glow'. A number of girls faced such severe skin conditions by now that even make-up couldn't cover their flaws. I was quite bewildered by the fact that Vasundra, who was the face of Fresh!, India's premier skincare company, had such a serious acne problem that she was forced to undergo a special treatment under Dr Kapoor's supervision, personally bearing all the expenses.

Dr Kapoor would come and look at our skin through an apparatus resembling a giant magnifying glass, and then prescribe something or the other. In most cases it was lacto-calamine lotion, whatever the severity of the case. She came in the day before the 'Miss Beautiful Skin' sub-contest and gave each of us a complimentary treatment, which basically comprised of a 'relaxing face-mask'. It was quite amusing to see Dr Kapoor shocked at the state of the girls' skin. She attributed their skin problems to the stress and pressure that had accumulated over the last month, but all of us knew that the true culprit was the make-up.

Much like everything else associated with this beauty pageant, our team of experts worked to brighten and polish the surface to make us all shine and dazzle on our big night.

They never looked beyond the superficial, at the nervousness and fear that was eating us up inside, at the vanity and jealousy that was disfiguring the beautiful faces, at the suspicion and malice that was arising as the pressure levels rose. What we all really needed was a moment. A moment of calm and peace to take in and digest what was going on around us. A moment to absorb all the thoughts and feelings that were racing through our minds. A moment to make peace with ourselves.

For me this was a time of revelation, a time of deep, serious thought. All of a sudden, as tensions grew high, I saw the worst come out in everyone. The ugly devil behind the charismatic facade was revealed. Everyone grew warier of each other and started guarding themselves and their possessions carefully. It was almost as if we were a team walking with our hands linked together, but at the last moment the line of trust was broken and everyone broke away, racing to the finish line, and in the process tripping each other up as much as they possibly could.

It wasn't only within the group that I saw this, it was with our trainers as well. The stress and pressure brought out the worst in Yasmeen. It was her job to choreograph a fabulous show, a show that would bowl over the crowds and leave them gaping. It had to be picture-perfect, every dainty step and every swing of the hip had to be perfectly coordinated. There could not be a single imperfection. It was her job to expunge all the flaws. The friendly,

179

trustworthy Yasmeen that we knew vanished as she whipped us into shape with her screams and shrieks, dragging our morale and spirits to an all-time low. The night before the big show, we rehearsed into the wee hours of the morning. She walked out on to the practice area, telling us that we were just not good enough, and how badly our performance would reflect on her capabilities as a top-rate choreographer. She told us that we were probably the least skilled and most dim-witted batch that this pageant had ever seen. We had all become accustomed to abuse, and we could take it, but not on the night before D-Day, when what we all needed was to be well-fed and tucked into our beds for a good night's sleep.

One night, engaged in a rare bout of friendly chatter with Yasmeen I asked, 'During your time as a model, the Miss Indian Beauty pageant used to be pretty big—did you ever feel the need to run for the contest?' She replied with a strange expression on her face, and a pimple on the right side of her face caught my attention. 'No, I did not. I never really needed it. I was getting good work, and didn't really need the name and fame attached to the pageant. Also, yaar, in my time, it wasn't that big a deal. I think it's a much bigger deal now.' This I found difficult to believe. If anything, the appeal of the pageant had only diminished in recent years. I figured Yasmeen knew more about the industry than I did, so I believed what she said with no second thoughts. It was only later that I found out, when I read

Jewels in the crown, a book about the Miss Indian Beauties of yesteryears, that Yasmeen Wadia had indeed run for the Miss Indian Beauty pageant, but had lost out to Suzy Sharma, a newcomer to the world of glamour.

Truly talented

The games had begun. The torch had been lit and the runners had started their journey. The competition had commenced for the various sub-categories that we would each contend for. From Miss Heavenly Hair to Miss Alluring Eyes, every aspect of our physical form was to be judged, the finest selected, and the very best awarded. Thus the flags were raised and we all went to war, to battle for the prize for best skin, smile and hair.

I was a bit unnerved when I found that there was to be a talent contest, more so because we were given all of two days to prepare for it. I racked my brains to figure out what I could do, even though I didn't really have any particular talent. I guess I was a fairly good squash player, but how does one display that in a talent competition? I was really the most ungraceful, non-artistic person I knew, and couldn't act, sing, dance or paint for a hoot. I was on the verge of not taking part—who needed the extra stress anyway—but didn't want to come across as an inept loser. Finally, I decided to play the flute, something I hadn't done for close to ten years. As a child I had been a fairly good flautist, and every once in a while I would pull out my flute, polish and admire it, and toot a tune just to make sure I could still produce a sound. There was one song that I had always played particularly well, and that was the theme song for the hit movie *Titanic*, which was quite popular and would definitely be a hit amongst the crowd. I had my parents hunt for my flute in the relics of my past and courier it to Mumbai. I practiced for all of two days. I was rather impressed with myself—I had managed to not only produce sound, but also music. To the ears of a non-musician it sounded pretty good, even though anyone more knowledgeable would have fainted at the untuned, off-key performance that I planned to give.

What 'talent' could a bunch of aspiring beauty queens possibly possess? You would be surprised. I was rather impressed with the talent show that was finally presented. Girls I never thought could possibly sing, sang sweet songs. Girls I could have never have imagined dancing swung their hips and shook their stuff like never before. Twenty out of the twenty-three girls took part in the talent round, and each one of them put up a good show in the three minutes that we were each given. Most of the girls either sang or danced. A few painted, recited poems which they had written, or gave acting performances. Some even went ahead with a fusion of a few of these things, reciting a poem, acting and singing, all in three minutes. Every performance that was given represented a facet of each girl's personality. Juhi sang a rather animated Punjabi song, Miriam put up a classical Kathak dance performance, and Poonam sang a Spice Girls song. Of course, some girls just took part for the heck of it and did things like whistling a song, or putting up a really clumsy dance.

Eight of the performances were selected for the final round, and I was fortunate enough to be one of the eight. Prachi sang an oldie Geeta Dutt song, Mrinalini put up a rather seductive performance, donning a short, black leather outfit and singing an Alicia Keyes song, Aashima painted an abstract figure in three minutes, Neelam sang the popular sufi song *Dum mast kalandar*, Stephanie put up a wacky act portraying an out-of-control hairstylist, and I played the flute. The final, winning act was a dazzling fusion Bharatanatyam performance by Vandana. Her performance called for a standing ovation. She deserved to win the title because she was truly talented. All of us had mustered up a talent at the last minute, though these couldn't honestly be called talents in the true sense of the word. Who was I kidding—I was no flautist. Vandana, on the other hand, was a professional Bharatanatyam dancer who not only danced fabulously, but taught as well. She was the only one of the lot who had true talent, and she rightfully won that crown.

So far we had all been part of a figurative race, but now we were part of a real race, to win the Miss Athlete title. As if making us pose, dance and smile wasn't enough, they were now making us race as well. I felt as if I had reverted back to my second-grade days, when we all stood in line, everyone trying to be a sly inch in front of the other, scurrying in the brown dirt, creating a momentary dust storm. This is exactly what we had to do to become Miss Athlete.

We arose at 5.30 a.m. and sleepily donned the ill-fitting Reebok outfits and uncomfortable sneakers that we had been given. We arrived at the venue, a dusty cricket ground, and were surprised to see an ambulance standing there, fully equipped with first-aid material. I guess you never knew with beauty queens, you had to careful, even if it was just one twenty-five-metre race. It was quite a simple procedure. We all raced in batches of five, and the winners were to then race again for the title.

I figured I would probably win, as after all I was athletics captain in high school, and really, what competition could a bunch of Miss Indian Beauty wannabes possibly pose? I was unpleasantly surprised when Stephanie overtook me and won the race by an inch. She went on to win the next race as well, and was declared Miss Athlete.

The two most coveted sub-categories of the Miss Indian Beauty pageant are Miss Body Beautiful and Miss Picture-Perfect. These are probably the two most important components of on-screen success. The morning of the contest, we all hesitantly got into our one-piece Speedo swimsuits which we had been given and proceeded to breakfast, though hardly anyone ate, making every effort at the last minute to appear as thin as they possibly could. Our judges for the contest were Atul Duggal, India's top photographer, and his protégé, the model Bhupen Patil. Atul had 'discovered' Bhupen in London and had brought him to India, propelling him to modelling success. Bhupen was now making his debut in the world of Bollywood, though I did not quite understand how, as he neither spoke nor understood Hindi.

This was to be the procedure: we had to walk down the ramp and then back again, so that the judges could get a good view of both our front and back. Then we had to go stand in front of the judges for closer inspection. It was really quite an uncomfortable experience, and I was dreading my turn on the ramp. Everyone felt much the same way, and each girl made her way down the ramp conscious of the stretch marks that ran down her backside, or the brown butt-cheeks protruding from the ill-fitting swimsuits, jiggling in a rather grotesque fashion. Mr Duggal and Mr Patel made their selections as each girl made her way down the ramp, and called upon the five that they had picked out. Everyone was quite shocked to see that Mrinalini was not a part of these five, as many girls had thought that she had the best body. Though she was the most curvaceous out of the bunch, I thought she could definitely have done with shedding a few pounds. In the world of modelling, curvaceous is not considered to be particularly beautiful. Apparently, it does not look very good on camera either. I was quite puzzled at some of the selections in the top five. I was bummed that my body wasn't considered 'beautiful' enough, but I guess everyone has a right to their own personal view of what a beautiful body is. However, I did notice that the selected five happened to be the bustiest of the group. Juhi finally emerged as the winner, which was an appropriate choice.

Before the next round of judging began, I asked Mr Duggal how he judged whether someone was photogenic. He explained that to be considered photogenic one had to look strikingly different on camera than in real life. The only way that this can happen is when you embrace the camera with arms wide open. You can only embrace the camera when you are not only comfortable with the way you look, but are truly, deeply and madly in love with yourself.

It was Neelam who finally won the title of Miss Picture-Perfect. She had dropped out of school after the tenth grade, because she was in love. A love so strong that it had pulled her away from her family and her home to Mumbai, to do ads. It was a love so strong that it had become close to an obsession. Neelam was in love with herself, and that is why she deservedly won the title of Miss Picture-Perfect.

What defines a Miss Congeniality? One would suppose that the girl who is the friendliest and most sociable of the lot would be considered the most congenial. It goes a bit deeper than that. It is human nature to develop a feeling of malice towards someone who is considered 'better' or more capable than yourself. Here, in the jungle of beauty, we were competing not for food or territory, but for a crown. Now we each had to cast our vote for the one among us who we thought was the nicest. Naturally, we each voted for the person we felt least intimidated by, who we felt posed no competition to us, and who had no airs about herself. The winner of this title was Harbjeet. Harbjeet hailed from the notorious city of Patna. This was the third year that she had attempted to be a part of the pageant. After being rejected at the pre-judging rounds two years in a row, she had now finally made it. It is interesting to examine what drives a small-town girl like Harbjeet, who has never left home even to attend college, to run for a pageant like Miss Indian Beauty.

She was the one who remained smiling up to the very end. She was the simplest of the lot, always modestly dressed, totally unpretentious. She was definitely not the most social—I barely spoke to her over that month—but she was the least threatening. Honestly, no one really thought she could win, and so Harbjeet was voted Miss Congeniality.

Next began the search for the girl who had a twinkle in her eye. Well, let's just say, the judges *did* find the girl with the twinkling eyes, but twinkling with tears, caused by an eye infection (blamed on Prince's make-up).

Poonam was a member of the desi crew. I never really understood why she was here—definitely not Miss Indian Beauty material. I had seen so many more capable candidates at the pre-judging. She was short, had a very ordinary face, and very sub-standard (if not poor) diction. During the Indira incident, Poonam and Shrutha (both nonentity contestants) had come to me and said that they were not 'allowed' to sign anything, because they were under contract to an agency that had paid for their expenses to the pageant. Their agent had told them to refrain from any activity that would result in signing papers. What agent, what agency, we never could figure out. On Sundays a short, shady old man wearing tight jeans, sporting platinum-blond streaks would come to visit Poonam and Shrutha at the hotel. I couldn't really figure out why these girls were here. Perhaps they wanted some fillers to keep the judging simple.

Poonam had been dealing with a minor eye infection ever since she had arrived, and had been to see the doctor on several occasions. It was a rather strange infection—it did not cause any redness or swelling, but led to a continuous formation of water in the eyes.

Our judges for this contest were Mrs Bharti, the managing director of Windsor Diamonds, a sponsor, and Monisha, an ex-Miss Indian Beauty contestant. I had no clue why she had been called in as a judge. The whole process was a bit awkward. We had to sit in front of two staring judges and look them straight in the eye without blinking. They then judged us on the luminosity of our eyes. It turned out that they mistook watery for sparkly, and Poonam, whose eyes were glazed with infection, went ahead to win the Miss Alluring Eyes title.

Neelam spoke incessantly about her beautiful hair. She spoke of how she had already made a few lakhs off her hair, and that her glossy mane was her biggest asset. She claimed that she had rejected many offers for hair products, and that she was in search of a contract that would pay her the asking price for buying the 'rights' to her hair. She had even gone as far as to say that she was the unambiguous winner of the Miss Heavenly Hair title. So when the sifting had taken place, and a few contestants were called for what we supposed was the 'final round', and Neelam was not called, she was in tears and had a mini-breakdown in front of the group. The judging for the hair, skin and smile titles were all taking place together, so we tried to reassure her that she could in fact have won, but she wouldn't listen to any of us. In between the hiccups and tears, I heard a few snatches. 'This was my dream, my life, and now it's over, I'm finished . . .'

The next morning, we could all tell that Neelam had cried the night away. Her bulbous eyes were swollen and barely discernable. We all tried to cheer her up, but to no avail, and in the end we gave up. Within a few days Neelam was back to her bubbly self, but we could see that somewhere within her, something had changed and there was still a bleeding wound that lay within her. That is, till the night of the finale, when Neelam found out that she had indeed won the Miss Heavenly Hair contest. To her this victory was like winning the Miss Indian Beauty title itself, and she let go of all inhibitions on stage. She had no qualms or worries, because she had already won what she had most wanted.

In India beauty is often associated with the colour of one's skin. It's a standard formula—the fairness of the skin is directly proportional to the level of beauty, so white equals beautiful. In many cases, the fairness of the skin is the sole determinant of female beauty. It is only now that things are changing. People are slowly starting to come to terms with the loveliness of dusky Indian skin, and are beginning to wipe off the layers of talcum powder and fairness cream to proudly reveal their true colour. This realization is slowly seeping into Indian hearts, but has not fully settled yet, so we had all thought that it was obvious that the girl with the fairest skin would win the title for Miss Beautiful Skin. The popular choices for this title were Shanaz and Aashima, and we were all surprised when Mrinalini, who was the darkest of the girls, was announced the winner. This was a good sign. People were beginning to look past mere colour, and deeper within to find true beauty.

The calm before the storm

It began the day before the pre-judging. The unnerving calm, and the uncomfortable silence. A painful hush had spread across the group, and the friendships that had been built seemed ready to collapse. Almost everyone resorted to their families and cellphones for comfort. By this time, almost everyone's families were in town. Some of the luckier ones, such as myself, had parents staying just a few floors above us at the same hotel, while other parents found more modest accommodations in guest houses and hotels spread over Mumbai's far-flung suburbs. A note of competitiveness had struck us all in the heart, and it was then that we truly realized that in just a few days, all but three of us would be back to square one, having come this far, standing at the threshold of glory. We would go back to the comfort and dullness of our respective homes whereas three, it could really be any three of us, would rejoice as the crowns sparkled on our heads. We realized that the friendships which we had built over the past month were like the rest of it, plastic, and at the end of it all, only the diamonds would speak. Everything else would vanish into thin air. We all took in the fact that in a few days our life as we knew it could change. The question of whether this change was for the better or the worse was never really asked, as in each girl's mind, the harsh shine of the diamonds overpowered everything.

For me, like everyone else, this was a time for contemplation, as the secret desire that I had nurtured for so many years was now going to come alive. It was me who would be walking down that ramp. I was going to be asked the questions; I was going to smile and wave at the crowd; it was me, Riya, contestant number seven, who could win that glittering crown, tears of joy forming in my eyes.

The pre-judging had begun, and only ten fortunate girls would make it through to the semi-finals. We wouldn't come to know who the final ten were till they were announced on stage, but it was on that ill-fated day that the elimination began. In many ways the pre-judging was more important than the finale, because it was during this time that we would first meet the panel of nine judges. It was at this time that first and possibly last impressions would be formed, as it was the only chance that we would get to converse with the judges one-on-one, if only for two minutes.

I wasn't the least bit nervous about pre-judging. I was eager for the end to approach. The production was finally drawing to a close, but the climax had not yet arrived. I was very eager to see how this drama would unfold, and on whose crest the coveted crown would finally rest. The activity of the past month had slightly dulled the shine of the contest, and I was anxious for it to end. At this point in the pageant, I felt more like I was part of the audience, an onlooker to the unfolding drama. I didn't share the emotions that the others felt. Being sleep-deprived and without ready access to caffeine, I was jittery and frazzled, but the looming, daunting image of the pageant was starting to diminish quickly in my mind. It just didn't seem like that big a deal anymore. It was then that I started enjoying it for what it was. Perhaps for the first time, I began to enjoy the process, silently laughing at the spectacle surrounding me, learning to enjoy the long periods of waiting, passing the hours observing people, and most of all, trying to let go of the scared little girl in me that lurked underneath the confident, arrogant veneer.

The thought of being in conversation with the judges, who without doubt would be eminent personalities, did not bother me in the least. If anything, I was looking forward to carrying out a conversation with these talented people. I took a deep breath. I decided that I was going to be calm, relaxed and confident. Just be yourself, I said to myself.

Hair and make-up had become a standard drill by now. The first ten girls went downstairs to begin their bedecking at dawn, followed by the rest, contestant-number-wise. For the pre-judging we sported a 'natural' look, with lots of petal-pink blush and glossy cherry lips. This pre-judging, similar to the round we had each gone through two months ago, comprised of two stages. The first was the swimsuit round, in which we wore the Speedo swimsuits which we had sported for the Miss Body Beautiful category. For the second round, we each wore the black 'cocktail outfit' which we had worn for the press conference. Once we had walked the ramp in these outfits, we were to then converse with each judge for exactly two minutes, in contestant-number order.

I was rather surprised at how calm all the girls were. I was expecting a minimum of three breakdowns, but the girls seemed surprisingly composed. An aura of confidence surrounded the group. I was excited, I was in need of some action, and was glad that the process was finally underway.

The morning flew by and before we knew it, twenty-three girls clad in swimsuits and bathrobes were herded together and marched off to be presented to the judges. It was when we all sat together, faces made up, in our body hugging swimsuits, waiting to meet the judges, that the nervousness finally set in. We had no idea who the nine judges would be, and were bursting with curiosity to find out which nine individuals would get to play God to us.

'Body oil, Riya?' 'Um, why not,' I said as I looked down at my well-moisturized legs. No harm in adding some glow, right? To lessen their anxiety, several girls frantically rubbed

196

oil on every imaginable part of their body, from their toes to their thighs, in an attempt to glow with health, well-being and confidence for the judges. I joined the crew. I heard many girls rehearsing imaginary conversations that they would hold with the judges, phrasing some rather cheesy lines to describe themselves. I was feeling it too, just a little bit, and was hoping and praying that I would be able to walk the ramp in a decent fashion in the rather uncomfortable shoes that we had each been given.

We were then taken to the backstage area of a temporary ramp, past a small room with nine chairs, a screen and a projector. Later we found out that before the pre-judging process Yasmeen had given a presentation on each one of us.

Before I knew it, I was walking down the ramp, doing the catwalk to an upbeat tune, balancing myself unsteadily on my three-inch heels, being looked up and down by nine pairs of critical eyes. Damn, that oil was not a good idea. I had lathered on so much that it had seeped into the soles of my shoes, and it was now getting difficult for me to walk as my feet slid in my shoes. I plastered a smile on to my face, struggling to disguise the uneasiness and discomfort that I felt. So many thoughts were flowing through my mind at that moment as I tried to connect familiar faces with big names, doing my best to appear as graceful and poised as I possibly could.

My turn was over in a flash, and before I could digest

what I had just been through, I had to rush backstage to change into my cocktail dress and shoes. I was back on stage in a jiffy, this time in my black cocktail dress. As I staggered down the ramp, I realized much to my misfortune that my right shoe had a cracked heel. Great, just what I needed, shoe woes to add to all the other ones. After the first nine of us had walked down the ramp, we each proceeded to 'chat' with each one of the nine judges.

First we met Mr Arvind Mahinder, an attractive man with earnest twinkling eyes and a laughing mouth, and a face framed by a neatly-trimmed steel-grey mane. He was clad in a simple grey suit and an expensive white shirt, without any embellishments save the Harvard class ring that rested on his right index finger. I had picked a favourite everything to prepare for my Q&A session, and if I had to pick my favourite judge, it would without a doubt have been Mr Mahinder.

'So you're a Wellesley girl—my sister graduated from there many years ago.' He smiled. Good, we were on the same wavelength. He knew where I was coming from.

'Sir, what do you do, exactly? We were not informed about who the judges are, for some reason.'

'I am the CEO of Mahinder Steel.'

'Oh, I see.'

I had heard a lot about this guy. He was supposed to be quite the dynamic businessman. As our conversation progressed, we found many common acquaintants, such as my uncle who ran the human resources department at his company. Through the course of our discussion, Mr Mahinder got progressively more curious as to why I was here. He asked me in a rather confused manner, 'What do your parents have to say about your Miss Indian Beauty aspirations?'

'Well, it's something that I have always wanted to do. They have always raised us to be independent individuals. They trust my decisions.'

The five-minute bell went off, and I had to move on to the next judge. As I got up, he extended his arm to shake my hand. 'Riya, what's the deal? Are you just here for shits and giggles?'

I didn't say anything. I just smiled back shyly. In a way, I took that statement as a compliment, because by saying this to me, he had taken me into confidence. He had told me in so many words what his perception of the contest was. I shook Mr Mahinder's firm hand and he gave me a knowing, somewhat mischievous smile, and I proceeded to the next judge.

I failed to charm Mr Sudhir Sippy, but his sandwich did not, and he seemed to be enjoying every bit of it, as he polished off an entire grilled cheese sandwich within the two-minute span of our conversation. Mr Sippy was a Bollywood actor of substantial fame who had slowly started fading away into oblivion as younger and more dynamic actors came of age in the industry. But he was holding on tight, doing flop film after flop film, struggling to revive the success of years gone by.

Mr Sippy and I did not really have much of a conversation, as he immediately launched into the merits and demerits of entering the world of glamour. I listened, smiling, straining to appear highly interested in what he had to say to me. He looked like a brawny rugby player, with his huge, sculpted chest, swollen biceps and tiny balloon head. The gruff, very masculine manner in which he spoke added to the image. He looked quite the seedy villain, straight out of the movies, in his black, rather ostentatious polyester suit, and generously gelled hair. After our rather flat, one-sided conversation, I went on to the next judge just as Mr Sippy was starting on his french fries.

Karen Kapadia was a Bollywood star, and it looked like she truly believed that she lit up the night sky with her beauty and panache, shining down on humanity. Many would have been quite intimidated by Miss Kapadia because of the haughty, arrogant, high-and-mighty image that she projected. To my pleasant surprise she was none of the above. This could also have been because she seemed to be rather consumed by a SMS conversation, and had a rather bored expression on her brightly painted face. If anything, she seemed to be a bit taken aback by the keenness that I displayed to strike up a conversation. Karen was the only judge with whom I faced an uncomfortable silence as we sat face-to-face with each other, mute, because she did not have anything to ask me. I did not see the conversation going anywhere, so I decided to take matters into my own hands. 'Are you excited to be judging this prestigious pageant?' I asked, and plastered one of the practiced smiles on my face. Karen seemed confused, perhaps at the audacity of my question. 'No, not really. I have actually judged one before, the time Tara Dutt and Priya Chopra won, so it's not a big deal . . . *at all*.' I didn't know what to say to that, so I just smiled. (Thank god for all that practice!) That was the end of our conversation. I got the feeling that Karen did not quite know what to make of me, a bold creature with an American accent who lived in Bhopal. As I left, she seemed to have completely forgotten about our conversation, and her face lit up as she proceeded to tap away on her mobile phone.

Next, I was to meet Craggy G. I was taken aback by him, by the way he looked, the way he was dressed, and most of all, by the questions that he proceeded to ask. When I first caught sight of him as I walked down the ramp, I was quite surprised by his presence. He stood out amongst the nine judges, in his bottle green shirt, tight black leather pants (it was summer, for God's sake) and spiky hair. He came off as somewhat slimy, with his sly smile and fidgety eyes. After the pre-judging, I heard rumours that he may have been intoxicated; some girls said that not only was he behaving intoxicated, but they had also caught a whiff or two on his breath.

I was taken aback when Craggy began to ask me one of those pseudo-psychological, mental-game type of questions. He looked me straight in the eye, giving me a wily smile, and asked me in a soft, singsong tone, 'Riya, tell me about yourself.'

'Well. . . . I go to college in Boston at Wellesley College, where I am an econ . . .'

He cut me off, still looking me straight in the eye. He waved his arms in the air, 'I don't want to know about what you do, I want to know about *you*, who you *really are*.'

I was confused—what the hell did he want me to say? 'Well, sir. . . .' I began, speaking without really thinking. 'I can say one thing about myself, that I am a passionate person.' I figured he would be into passion and all that. 'I don't do many things in life, but when I choose to do something, I give it my all, and when I am truly devoted to something or someone, it is impossible to pull me away.' He smiled at me, revealing his yellowed teeth. I guess that meant he liked my answer.

'So tell me, pretty girl, what is your mantra for life?'

'Hope for the best, but expect the worst.'

'Hmm, does that mean that you are a pessimist?'

'No, not really, it means that I believe in fate, in destiny . . .'

Once again he smiled that creepy smile. All in all, I felt as if I had handled this psychoanalysis pretty well. I did not lose my cool, and did not appear cornered. I had nimbly escaped the trap that Craggy G had attempted to set for me, that too with a certain amount of grace and style.

Next, I was to be confused by a diminutive, elfin gentleman wearing a dazed look, clad in his tweed suit and plaid socks. It was much later, on the night of the contest, that I found out that he was Jay Vimal, the editor-in-chief of the *Indian Standard*. The dazed, sleepy look that Mr Vimal held turned to confusion when he met me. I took complete control over the conversation as Mr Vimal gave me the freedom to rattle on about myself, and I really felt the need to do so after the mental exercise I had been through with Craggy G. I told the wizened Mr Vimal all about myself, about the thesis that I was working on, about my keen interest in the world of finance, my passion for development . . . the more I spoke, the more confused he became. All of a sudden he interrupted my prattle. 'Why the *heck* are you here, young lady?' I was taken aback. I paused. 'You see, sir, I have wanted to be a Miss Indian Beauty since I was a little girl. I tried to ignore this fledgling hope, but it grew over the years till I couldn't ignore it any more.' I added a bit hesitantly, 'When I grow old, I don't want to bear any regret in my heart. I need to get it out of my system, and right now is the time.'

I was completely honest with him, and with the rest of the judges for that matter. In retrospect maybe I shouldn't have been. I was such an idealist. If I told everyone that I aspired to be an actress, maybe they would have thought I was more 'serious' about the title. I had thought of this entire process as a fair game. I had believed that the one who truly deserved the title, had the capability to represent the country in the best possible manner, would win. I had thought that a Miss Indian Beauty was the epitome of the Indian woman. She was beautiful, intelligent and cultured. She held the ideals of the country close to her heart, and practiced what she preached with unprecedented grace and charm. I never thought of a Miss Indian Beauty just as an aspiring model, actress or entertainer. This is what the pageant had become, and it is only now that I realize how quixotic my thoughts were.

On the board of the Miss Indian Beauty jury, among celebrated actors, illustrious industrialists and savvy socialites, there is always one ex-Miss Indian Beauty. This year it was Celine Chandra who, after winning the Miss Indian Beauty title, had taken the well-traversed path to Bollywood and had caused quite a sensation with her audacious performances. She had kept the Miss Indian Beauty legacy alive, but had given a new twist to the tale with her rather revealing and controversial performances.

Celine was an ice maiden and her luminous eyes, made even more chilling with the help of brilliant-blue contact lenses, stared me straight in the eye. Her face was frozen with concentration as she drew up a mental analysis of each contestant. She stared at me intently for a long time, and it was almost as if she was trying to crack me open through her steely glare. I smiled at her motionless visage, hoping to extract a smile from that frosty face. 'Gosh, that cheese sandwich looks so delicious,' I said with a playful smile, pointing to the untouched sandwich lying next to her. She smiled back. She looked me deep in the eye. I got a tad worried. She looked so serious that I took a deep breath and prepared myself for a killer question.

'Riya, tell me, was there any *bitchiness* amongst the girls? Were there any catfights?'

I tried hard to conceal the smirk that was forming on my face as I tried to answer the question with a straight face. As I rose from my chair, I thought to myself, this was to be expected. She was a Miss Indian Beauty after all.

I was then due to meet Sharmila Ray. Mrs Ray led a fabulous life. Having started out as a society columnist, she eventually rose to be the editor of *Gloss* magazine and then launched a wildly successful career as a writer. Her first few best-selling novels found their roots in Page 3 parties and diamond-studded evenings. She was a socialite par excellence and had done well for herself by penning down her social experiences into satirical novels. I was a fan of her lifestyle and flamboyance.

I was expecting Mrs Ray to be vivacious and animated, but was surprised at her quiet yet elegant aura. Her whimsical, twinkling eyes were set in a gentle face, subtly creased with the lines of age. We had a pleasant conversation, nothing more or less than that. She asked me about my family and my background, and I was surprised to find out that she had grown up in similar circumstances to myself. Her father was an IAS officer as well. I rose from my chair when the bell sounded. On leaving, as I shook her hand, she gave it a gentle, deliberate squeeze before saying goodbye.

The next judge was quite easy to deal with. Priya Batra juggled a number of professions. She was an actress, a socialite and even had her own show on television. She was the only judge who had bothered to prepare questions for us.

'So Riya, what are the biggest difficulties you face on stage?'

Well, that was obviously quite clear from my tottering walk. 'You see Priya, I have never been a model, and the catwalk is very new to me. I am still not very comfortable on the ramp. Also,' I added shyly, 'I am just not used to wearing high heels.'

'They're such a pain! I am such a fan of chappals,' she said enthusiastically. The alarm went off, and I went on to face the final judge.

The last judge that I faced was the sternest of the lot. Ravi Singh Marwar was a marksman who hailed from the army and had been in the headlines recently for winning an Olympic medal. After the animated conversation I had just had with Priya Batra, I was taken aback by Mr Marwar's expressionless visage and militaristic style of questioning.

Mr Marwar would pose a question, and just as I started to reply, before I could even finish a sentence, he would cut me off and shoot off another question, completely disjointed from the first. Throughout our five minute conversation he maintained that poker face, and I was unable to extract a smile from this stony man. Mr Marwar surely used this adroitness at making me uncomfortable, no doubt derived from his marksmanship, to tackle this situation. I shot back answers with deftness, but these answers were perhaps not the *correct* ones. I said what I truly felt, and not what was perhaps the expected answer. Mr Marwar looked me straight in the eye. His pencil-thin moustache twitched slightly. My fake eyelashes were bothering me, but I feared that touching my face in front of this stern man could have been construed as bad manners. He asked me in a thick accent, 'What are your thoughts about the Indian woman?'

'Sir,' I began, 'the true representation of the Indian woman is not the cosmopolitan, denim-clad, internet-savvy individual that one finds in the metros, she is the bindi-bearing, sindhur-wearing woman that you find existing in the villages in the heart of India. That woman is still tackling the atrocities of dowry, infanticide and sexual abuse. That Indian woman is lagging far behind and has miles to go and numerous battles to fight before she can be proclaimed aware and equal.' This was a sensitive issue for me, as I had worked with women's grassroots organizations in the past, and I had pretty strong views on this matter. In the intensity of my mini-speech I failed to remember that I was running for a beauty pageant, where *conventional* and *conformist* were the key words to success. The alarm bell sounded and I rose to leave, past ten anxious girls frantically rehearsing practiced lines as they awaited their moment to be judged. I felt as if I was returning home after a long and tiring battle, but I was confused, as I did not know whether I had won or lost. I once again felt that unsettling feeling of doubt and insecurity, but I ignored it. My father's words resounded in my head. 'Beta, when you are running a race, always keep your eyes on the finish line. The minute you look back to see if you are winning, you lose the race.'

I resolved to keep my eyes on the finish line.

The final act

We were finally approaching the end. For the past one month the drama had been slowly building up, and now the final and most important act was to be played, before the curtain finally went down. For three girls, this would be the beginning of a life-long journey, but for the other twenty it would be the end of a childhood dream. I felt as if I was on the edge of my seat, watching a thriller movie, nervously biting away at my fingernails, waiting for the climax so that I could sit back, relax and enjoy the popcorn.

On the morning of the pageant, all the girls went to get their hair and make-up done. There was an unnatural silence. In their minds they could all hear the distant yet crystal-clear din of the approaching storm. They ate their last breakfast of fruits and nuts, and perused the day's newspapers more thoroughly than they ever had before. As they sipped on their last glasses of vegetable juice, carefully, for fear of disturbing their make-up, they dreamt and waited for their big moment.

It was surreal. I was calm and collected, but at the same time excited and scared at the prospect of giving the biggest performance of my life. I had dreamt of this moment for so long, and now it was finally happening. I felt I had relapsed into my schooldays, and as if I was facing my twelfth grade board exams after the one-month-long preparation leave that we got. Like I had always done before an exam, I prepared myself mentally, physically and, most importantly, emotionally. Instead of churning mathematical formulae through my mind, I churned quotations and phrases. I had always believed that I would perform my best in an exam if I was in complete physical comfort. I would wear my most comfortable underwear beneath my neatly ironed uniform, and would always spray on some mosquito repellant to avoid the possibility of insects distracting me during the exam. In this case it was a bit different. How could I possibly be comfortable with a beehive bun sitting on my head, wearing a skintight gown or a five-kilogram salwar kameez, and to top it all off, three-inch heels? I did all that I possibly could to make myself comfortable, pasting insoles and cotton balls on to the soles of my shoes to make them as comfortable as they could possibly get. Emotional preparation was perhaps the most strenuous. I played every possible situation over in my mind a million times, from being cast out in the first round or final round, to my name being called out as the winner or runner-up. I rewound and fast-forwarded each situation again and again, in an attempt to steel myself and develop immunity to any pain and sadness that an unfamiliar situation might evoke.

We loaded into our Miss Indian Beauty mobile for the last time, and for the entire length of the thirty-minute ride to the venue, there was pin-drop silence. The MMRDA grounds, the popular venue for most big entertainment events, had changed overnight. For the past week we had been going through rigorous practice sessions in this dusty ground. We had spent many hours here, and each one of us knew the grounds and stage inside out. Tonight, it had been transformed from the dusty, grimy cricket field that we knew, holding a half-constructed stage along with mounds of trash and its own family of stray dogs, into a dream world. The stage had been lit in shades of pink and blue, with opulent glass fittings, the most impressive of which was a glittering crystal chandelier. Shiny, colourful banners screaming out the names of the sponsors and their products were displayed everywhere, the most predominant of which were the baby-pink Fresh! banners shouting the pageant slogan. In a matter of seconds we were transported from our pensive world of thoughts and aspirations into a beehive of activity as we were rushed into the green room to begin getting dressed for the pageant.

For the first of the three sequences we wore long, flowing evening gowns in shades of orange and pink. Our outfits went well with the ambience of the stage, and presented a very pretty picture. Each one of us had been given a 'helper' to assist us in changing our outfits. We were helped into our gowns and then rushed into the jewellery room, where we were decorated with some rather magnificent diamond jewellery. I felt like a princess out of a fairy tale, with the lovely gown, the beautiful jewellery, the whole world's eyes upon me. Within moments we were backstage. For the first sequence we were to walk out and do some simple choreography to the 'Roop' number, the title song for the pageant. This would be the first time that we would step on to the stage, and I eagerly waited for the familiar tune to begin. This was the moment I had been waiting for—I would set that stage on fire, and I was going to give the performance of a lifetime. The music cue began. I held my breath to make my stomach look as flat as possible in the ultra-clingy gown. I stepped on to the stage wearing my brightest smile, ready to face the lights, cameras and action. It was amazing to see everything condense so rapidly into the span of a two-hour show. When I stepped on to the stage I was overwhelmed by the vastness of the audience, the bright lights, the cameras, the grandeur of the entire scene and, most of all, the panel of judges.

We exited almost as quickly as we had walked on to the stage. I hadn't had time to feel anything. It was over. Just like that. Before I knew it, we were back in the green room, struggling to get into the outfits for our second sequence, while the crowd was entertained by the Bombay Rockers, the 'in' band of the season.

For the second act I wore a lovely one-shouldered embroidered kurta with a sequinned churidar. We all looked wonderful in that second sequence, glittering in the shimmery pastel blues and pinks that we donned. I don't think I have ever worn such an elaborate outfit in my life, and I felt a bit weighed down in the heavy kurta and opulent jewellery. Once again we were all backstage, our hearts fluttering at the thought of the impending announcement.

It was time for the ten semi-finalists, chosen by the judges the day before, to be announced. I felt unnaturally calm as I waited to walk on to the stage again. The jazzy, upbeat music started and I walked on to the stage, more confidently than I had ever done before, swinging my hips, my arms on my waist, my head held up high. We assembled ourselves in a row as the music faded away, and we heard the hosts speak of the training program and the sponsors. I held my breath and silently prayed to God. Underneath our silken drapes, Miriam and I clasped our hands together.

It felt like a slow motion slap in the face. 'Ladies and gentleman, the moment that we have all been waiting for! It is time to declare the ten semi-finalists of the evening . . . Contestant #1: Amisha! Contestant # 2: Aparita! Contestant # 6: Vandana! Contestant #8: Miriam!' I let her fingers go as her face lit up and she walked to the front of the stage. I did not really hear anything after that. The smile that had been plastered on my face was harshly wiped away. I kept my hopes up till the very end. Perhaps they had missed my name on the list, maybe they had made a mistake in the scores. I was hoping fervently that someone would rush on to the stage and say that there had been a mistake.

It wasn't until the very last name had been called and I had made my exit that I realized that I hadn't been chosen. I was in a peculiar state of shock. It was numbing. It was almost as if I had been expecting this defeat, yet I couldn't digest the fact that it was all over for me. I wouldn't be answering any questions. There would be no crown for me. I looked around at the other faces, at the girls who, like me, hadn't been chosen. The hosts continued to talk. 'Congratulations on making it this far. It is an achievement . . .' The hosts proceeded with empty words of consolation, the contestants' smiles still plastered on to their faces. Their quivering eyes gave them away. Underneath those smiles, underneath all the diamonds and make-up, there were thirteen little girls who were crying their hearts out, staring at the shattered dream that lay in front of them.

That was the end of that. I was stunned by the indifference I felt, even as I tried to muster up some sort of emotion within myself. It didn't hurt even a little bit, it really didn't. In a way I was pissed off, because failure was new to me. Back in the green room, everyone seemed surprisingly calm. I proceeded to change into my next outfit.

I had plenty of time before I was to be back again on stage. I hadn't won any of the side contests, nor did I have to answer any questions. I could just chill backstage and enjoy the show. At one point I seriously thought of leaving, especially as the zipper of my last outfit was broken, and no replacement had been found yet. I was a sore loser, but not *this* sore. I couldn't leave. Since I was here, I might as well wrap things up properly.

Most of the ten girls who had been chosen came as a surprise to all of us. Amisha, Aparita, Vandana, Miriam, Neelam, Prachi, Preeti, Juhi, Sonia and Mrinalini. Aparita, Neelam and Juhi were completely unexpected, even Vandana and Prachi were dark horses. I was surprised by the absence of Aashima's name on the list. I was wallowing in my defeat, and didn't really pay attention to the questions that the contestants were being asked until I saw Miriam's turn approach. I wanted Miriam to win. Someone had to win, and if not me, I wanted her to own that crown. I rushed to the television just as she picked her card, and Celine Chandra began her question. 'If you had to tell one lie to win the contest, what would it be?' It was a weird question. To answer this question at the spur of the moment was quite a challenge. Miriam was the most capable of the chosen ten to tackle this answer. She began, 'The biggest lie would be that there are twenty-three winners . . . uh, sorry,' I saw a sheepish smile form on her face.

'Shit, come on, Miriam,' I said to myself. 'Come on.'

215

She had fumbled. It was just for a second, and she recovered.

'The biggest lie would be that there are three winners and twenty losers, when in fact, despite defeat, we have learnt so much through this entire process that each one of us is a winner at heart.' Despite her well-worded answer, she had fumbled, and that had finished it for her. In a way I was relieved. In times of competition, especially when diamonds are involved, the ugly green monster called jealousy emerges within every woman, and it was no different with me. Even though I did want Miriam to succeed, I swear I did, I couldn't bear the thought that she had made it and I had not.

Miriam returned, and as she changed into her third outfit, I reassured her. 'Come on yaar, your answer was good. It was a tough question, you will *definitely* make it.'

I knew that she did not stand a chance. She looked really nervous. I hadn't ever seen her like this.

Miriam rushed out of the green room, where a camera crew had assembled. The ten semi-finalists were gathered together, and the five who had made it to the next round were announced. The camera crews flocked around them to catch their reactions. Amisha, Neelam, Prachi, Preeti and Mrinalini were to go on to the next round. Miriam returned. She looked peaceful. Poor Juhi wasn't chosen, and on returning she had something that resembled an asthma attack. She recovered soon enough, as the ousted girls gathered around the television set to see what would happen next.

The chosen five stood at their podiums, pens in hand, waiting to scribble down the answer to the question that would decide their future. 'OK girls, this is it. Ready or not, here it is . . .' screeched the overexcited host. 'What would you do the save the world?' God, this had to be the flakiest question ever. I cannot believe that the most clichéd beauty pageant question of all time had been asked. The seconds ticked away as the five girls frantically scribbled down their answers. The timer went off, and pens were put down. The answers were read. Out of the selected five, I really wanted Preeti to win. Not that I had ever really liked the girl, she was really weird, but I felt that she would do justice to the title. She would represent the country much better than the other four.

The answers were read out. Like the question, they were all clichéd and trite. Amisha responded very confidently, the perfect Miss Indian Beauty smile plastered on her face. 'I would propagate love and harmony throughout the universe and expunge it of all lust, hatred, jealousy, malice and crime.' It was unlikely that Amisha would ever try to do all that, but the answer *sounded* good. She had obviously mugged up that list of synonyms and antonyms that Emma had given us. Preeti said something which made no sense, that she wanted to create a love machine or some such thing. Prachi even went to the extent of saying that she would like to create a device to sense jealousy and resentment. Honestly, is this what they would do to save the world! The only semi-intelligent answer was Mrinalini's. 'I would like to create a cure for cancer, the disease which snatches away so many innocent lives, just like it did my granny's.' At least this was something concrete. I don't know if bringing in the granny was such a good idea, though.

Neelam answered with a little too much enthusiasm. Even on TV, I saw some spit spewing out of her mouth and on to the jacket of the host. He didn't seem to like it very much. Probably not what he expected from a beauty queen. Her answer was hackneyed, and didn't really make too much sense, but it was said with panache and confidence. 'I would give all the starving children of this world food to fill their stomachs. After all, children are the future!'

We waited for the results.

I walked on to the stage for the very last time. I was wearing a flowing silk skirt with an ill-fitting kurta that had been dug out at the last minute. We looked dazzling for the finale, clad in white, black and gold. The music began and I walked out. Never before had I been so confident on the ramp. I did the catwalk to near perfection. This was the only time throughout that one month that I let myself go completely.

I held myself up high, took every step perfectly, not once staggering in the three-inch heels. As I strutted past the judges, I threw them evil looks. We once again assembled together, waiting for the three names to be called. This time I felt no nervousness, just deep curiosity. The climax to the drama that I had been a part of for the past month would finally unfold.

As I stood there waiting for the three names to be announced, the bubble suddenly went 'pop'. I felt as if I was in a daze, watching a cheesy television show rather than being *in* it. The setting of the show, which at first had seemed so grand, now felt so small. The stage felt tiny, the fixtures gaudy, the judges obscure, and the audience insignificant.

'Miss Earthly Indian Beauty is . . . Neelam!' She came forward to receive her crown with a look of disbelief on her face. Tears streamed down her face. The firecrackers went off, and a shower of rose petals began. It all felt so tacky and tawdry. I stood there clapping. With zeal and gusto, the host called out, 'Our World Miss Indian Beauty . . . is . . . Mrinalini!' She came forward to receive her crown, her jaw hanging open. It looked so passé from where I stood. The ex-World Miss Indian Beauty, in her tasteless outfit, came forward to hand her the bouquet of roses, placing the crown on her head. Beneath the facade she simmered—the torch of glory that she had held for the last year now had to be passed on.

'Now, the moment we have been waiting for all evening . . . the Miss Universal Indian Beauty, the most beautiful woman in India today, is . . . Amisha, contestant # 1!'

The corny *Star Wars* music started playing. Some very loud fireworks went off, unnervingly close to where the judges sat clutching their ears. The ex-Miss Universal Indian Beauty, Tania, came forward with two young children, handed Amisha the roses, and gave her congratulatory hugs and kisses.

Prachi and Preeti stood at their positions, clutching each other, tears forming in their eyes. They had been so close. They had seen the crown and the glittering diamonds so close, so tantalisingly close, and now they had been callously snatched away from them.

Just like that, in the snap of a finger, it was over, and I was exactly where I had started off from. Perhaps even worse off than before, thanks to the embarrassing publicity I had received from this pageant. I was now a part of the dead sea of Miss Indian Beauty girls, where the corpses of losers are flung. If lucky, they are fished out by some model coordinator or the other and placed back on earth. I went back to the green room, where parents flooded in to console their teary daughters. Among the sea of distressed parents stood three sets of enthralled parents, overwhelmed by all the media attention. I was in a pensive mood. I tried to look within myself and tear out any shreds of sadness and regret. I felt numb to all emotion. It felt much like when I had played competitive squash—intense while it lasts, but as soon as it was over I acknowledged that it was just a game.

I read the SMS that my parents had sent me as soon as I was out: 'Baby, no matter what, you are still the centre of our universe.' I touched the bun that Heather, our sweet hairstylist, had spent an hour on, whispering in my ear, 'I am giving you a special bun. I will take my sweet time on your hair, because I know you are going to win.'

I glanced at the SMS that my teenage cousin from Lucknow had sent me. 'Riya didi, the judges were stupid, you were the best, and still are the best for us.' It was these things that brought tears to my eyes. It was the thought that people had hopes for me, and I had failed them. My brain cried out to me, it cried out that it was only a beauty pageant, and that I didn't need a panel of judges to rate me. I knew who I was and what I was, and I didn't need diamonds to tell me that I had been successful. I had my strength to carry me through.

Of thorns and tiaras

The sweet taste of alcohol. The even sweeter taste of bread. The sweetest taste of chocolate. I stood with my painted face and the bun which threatened to collapse, at the after-party of the pageant. It was compulsory to attend. I stuffed my face with food as ruthlessly as I possibly could, not caring about lipstick or cameras. It felt good. I was surprised at the Page 3 people that this party had managed to attract. Then again, there is not much else happening around town on a Sunday night, and for party people, any occasion is an opportunity for revelry.

I had quite a few engaging conversations that evening, but a few stand out in my mind. It was here that I got the chance to talk to the judges as ordinary people, sans the fear of being judged.

The wine had gotten to me, and I was having a lengthy conversation with one of the judges, Mr Vimal. He was actually a pretty cool guy when he wasn't a judge. 'Tell me,' I said, a bit unsteady on my heels, 'Why didn't I make it to the top ten?' He looked at me through his tortoise-shell glasses and smiled. 'I marked you highly, you impressed me. But one never knows what happens, there are eight other judges after all.'

'You know what . . .' I put the wine glass down. I was getting a bit woozy. 'I think the final three choices were wrong. I promise you, it's not the sting of defeat speaking. I am speaking from a crystal-clear, razor-sharp, analytical economics perspective.' As I told him this, he shook his head and gave me a sad smile. 'Riya, God knows what happens at these beauty pageants. They have been asking me to be a judge for three years now. I finally came here kicking and screaming.' There was nothing I could say to this. I returned the smile.

I spoke to a man with a hat. He told me that he was looking out for me today. He was looking for the arrogant, beautiful girl who he knew would never make it. I asked him why, and how he knew this. He told me, wearing a shrewd smile, his astute eyes sparkling in the cloud of cigar smoke that surrounded him, that girls like me could never win. I had a life, and a good life at that. This crown was given to someone who desperately needed it. It was given to someone who desperately wanted it. Someone who had dreamt of it night after night, who would give up anything and everything for the diamonds. I didn't need it.

Hell, I didn't even want it that badly. The tears had failed to appear when it was snatched away from under my nose. It had been a dream for me, but truthfully, and absolutely honestly, it had only been half-dream. Half-dreams are a deception, he said. They shine for a moment and you run towards them, but just as you are running towards them, they fade away into oblivion and you stop.

As I stood sipping on more wine (I really should have stopped), staring at the ocean, oblivious to the harsh music, a wizened old man with a camera around his neck came up to me and asked to take my photograph. He asked me, 'Young lady, you are beautiful, what did you win tonight?' I gave him a smile and replied, 'Nothing, sir. I didn't even make it to the top ten.' He replied with an exclamation of surprise. 'My oh my, a beautiful young lady like yourself . . .'

'I don't regret it. Really. If anything, I am happy. It would not have been fair if I had won, I have no value for the crown. I would do it no justice whatsoever.' He smiled sadly and told me, 'Young lady, I have been watching this contest for years. I was the one who took the black-and-white photographs of the Miss Indian Beauties in the Hanging Gardens, to send to the Miss Universal Beauty pageant.' He paused for a moment and then began again. 'You see, it just isn't that simple. After all, it is a commercial affair. If girls like you make it to the top ten, there will be complications. It has to be made simple and clear for the judges.'

Someone once told me that if something has to happen, the entire universe will conspire to make it happen. If something is not destined to occur, the universe will play ugly games to stop it from happening. Now and again I wonder. I wonder why I didn't make it to the top ten. There was no reason why I shouldn't have been there. I don't mean to sound vain, but looking at it from a physical point of view, I probably had a better face/body combination than half the girls in the top ten. From day one, all our instructors had told us that it would be a neck-to-neck competition between each one of us. I had always been pretty confident of making it to the top ten. Maybe it was my lax attitude that led to my defeat, but how could the judges gauge that in the two minutes that they had with me? Maybe I failed to make a good first impression when I walked down that ramp. But I had a chance to redeem myself in the interview session. Even if I did not appear confident on the catwalk, at least when the judges spoke to me at the pre-judging, I must have radiated the confidence that I felt within. Perhaps they misjudged my confidence for arrogance. I still haven't completely figured it out.

I woke up at daybreak the next morning, as my body was accustomed to the early morning rise. I couldn't believe that it was all over. At breakfast, the atmosphere was morose as twenty girls munched on profusely buttered toasts. Overnight, the three winners had changed. They kept much to themselves, talking amongst each other about the bright futures that lay ahead of them, planning their diet for the next month, talking about the various shoots that were coming up. All of a sudden there was a bridge that divided these girls from the rest of us, and no one wanted to, or had the courage to cross that bridge. We were all going home, back to where we had come from, taking with us only pieces of our shattered hopes and bitter-sweet memories.

I went home to Bhopal the very next day, reliving every moment over and over again in my head. It was difficult to let go. The memories were so vivid in my mind. It wasn't just me; everyone felt that way. In those initial days we found solace in each other. It was as if we had been transported to an alien world for a month, and been returned to earth with a bump. No one could really understand what we had been through, physically and emotionally, except perhaps each other. Miriam and I spoke to each other every day for the next week. Gradually we settled back to our daily lives. Within a month, the pageant seemed like the distant past, a past which had nevertheless touched the present for so many of us.

At the end of it all, after the cameras had stopped flashing, after the tears had been shed, after our bags had been packed, and each of us had bid the other farewell, we all wondered. It was as if we had been left hanging. After an entire night of discussions and midnight-snacking on the junkiest food on the in-room dining menu, we were more confused than ever before. Even though the month had begun in doubt with the Indira incident, in the chaos and rush of activity, the thought had never again crossed our minds. We never wondered about it any further. To be honest, we really didn't have the time to (and maybe some of us didn't have the brains, either), but now, as we waited at the reception, checking out of the pageant, checking out of the dream, clearing up all the traces, ready to go back to where we had come from, we all felt as if we had been left hanging. It did not feel as if everything had been neatly swept up in a pile and tossed into the recycle bin of our mind, where the same thoughts would be processed over and over again, until a day came when they would finally be purged.

We all felt as if there was a layer of fog surrounding everything. There was no evidence, just a feeling, a feeling that burned within twenty unsatisfied hearts.

I had heard from various people—ex-boyfriends, parents and friends of those who had participated, and contestants from earlier years who had lost—that the Miss Indian Beauty contest was fixed. Of course I realized that this statement could just as easily have come from bitter experience, and this was a way of justifying failure and calming the flaming, fast-swelling insecurity of defeat.

Now, I began to wonder.

Hours of discussion, hours of contemplation, and many sleepless nights later, I too felt that the suspicions of all these people weren't completely unfounded.

In my mind there were three reasons, and three reasons only. Three reasons that I found after clearing my thoughts, picking up the scattered pieces, and clearing up the fog. All of this could very well have been a figment of my rather over-active imagination, or it could even be chance. That is for you to decide.

The first reason was Mr Parek's psychoanalysis, the day before the pre-judging. As an organizer, what business did he have judging us in such a manner? After all his interactions were over, he met us as a group and asked us to write down on a piece of paper the names of two girls who we expected to win, and before submission, a chaperone checked to make sure we had not written our own name. To what avail was this process? I never did understand. Perhaps this was the only conceivable way to establish popular opinion.

Reason number two is what got me thinking in the first place. Miriam, who had made it to the top ten, had revealed this to me, and I then confirmed this with a few of the semi-finalists.

Each of the judges asks a question to each of the ten contenders. Which judge asks which contestant what question is meant to be random. The contestant normally

228

draws the name of the judge from a stack of cards. Miriam later told me that she was very surprised that she had not been asked to pick a card with the name of the judge who then proceeded to ask her question. Instead, the host had *handed* her a card which had already been marked with her contestant number and the name of a judge.

What made it even stranger was that we had thought (quite naturally) that the judges would choose the question that they would then ask. We later found out that it was Mr Parek who had set the ten questions which the judges had finally posed to the contestants.

I only realized the third reason after very, very careful analysis. The questions posed to each of the ten contestants seemed to be 'set' to the answering capacity of each contestant. For example, Juhi, who had openly expressed her lack of knowledge of politics several times, had been asked a question based on just that. Ironic. The question posed to Amisha, the winner, was 'If you were a message on a t-shirt, what would you be?' This was the very first question listed on the Q&A book that each one of us knew inside out. It was the only question of the ten that came from our handbook. The question posed to Mrinalini, the first runner-up, was based on a very popular topic of discussion during that time (the whole casting couch, invasion of privacy issue), which was the topic that was perhaps the most extensively discussed during Mr Parek's Q&A session. Neelam, who was quite the bimbette and who would flounder when posed with even the most basic questions, was asked a question of unbelievable simplicity, far simpler than the rest of the nine questions. She was asked, 'What is your favourite book?' Needless to say, she had gone into the pageant with an answer safely mugged up to this question.

These were my three reasons, dear reader, this is what I made of it, and now I leave it to you to draw your own conclusions.

You see, it was a world of plastic, a world where flaws are covered up by make-up, a world where all you see is the glittering surface, where the cracks are perfectly concealed by the glint of the diamonds, where beautiful words are said that have no meaning, where tales are woven, but have no substance, where the world appears as a dazzling red rose with an intoxicating fragrance that draws you closer and closer. You are charmed by the radiant colour and sweet scent, but as you move forward to touch it, you pull back at the excruciating pain, and the colour of the blood that gushes out of a tiny yet agonizing wound is red, a red much, much deeper than the red of the rose.

This, my friends, was a world where things are really not what they appear to be, and I attempted to reach beneath the glistening surface but pulled back, far back, when it struck me with a tiny thorn that caused great pain, but if only for a moment.

Postscript

I have managed to keep in touch with a few of the Miss Indian Beauty girls, and it is interesting to take a look at how their lives have unfolded after the pageant.

I talk to Miriam on a regular basis. After the pageant, she realized that she wanted to do more with her life. She is moving to Mumbai from Dubai to model and work as an RJ for Radio One.

On her return to Bangkok, Aashima went into a mild state of depression. She is now moving to Mumbai to fulfill her Bollywood dreams, while embarking on a search for an eligible bachelor.

Stephanie is back to her regular life in Mumbai, dabbling in the world of fashion. Last I heard, she had joined Farah Khan's famed dance troupe for a stint as a professional dancer.

Harbjeet returned home to Patna to fame and glory. Lalu Prasad Yadav had caught wind of her Miss Indian Beauty experience and wanted to personally congratulate her for bringing Bihar to the forefront of fashion. I am currently helping her with her resume, as she is contemplating a career as an air hostess.

Shortly after the Miss Indian Beauty pageant Sonia took part in the 'Miss Tourism' pageant (whatever the hell that is) and won. She is now busy promoting tourism in South-East Asia. She is considering moving to Mumbai, where there is apparently more 'work'.

I recently attended the India Fashion Week (as a part of the audience), where I saw Juhi on the ramp. I later saw her at the after-party, quite intoxicated, on the shoulder of a man sporting a Rolex.

Six girls from the desi crew signed a contract with Air India, which allows them to work as cabin crew and do some modelling on the side. They are now in Mumbai, training for this position.

Unfortunately for Mr Parek, none of the chosen three won the international crowns. I see them in random articles now and then, as they busy themselves for the next few months before a new set of girls will be crowned. When I met Mrinalini a few days ago, she looked rather unhappy, and complained of being broke as she hadn't yet received any of her cheques. We had all been asked to sign a contract the day before the finale, which forbade the winners from endorsing any products other than the sponsors'. All the three winners were bound to give thirty per cent of their earnings to the sponsoring group for the next six years. This contract was causing Mrinalini a certain amount of grief as she searched for ways to earn a living.

Now and again I see the other girls on TV on some random

232

music video or the other. As for me, well, I intend to pack up and head to NYC for a short stint on Wall Street, after which I will be back at Wellesley College for my final year. I intend to continue my writing in the hope that people will read what I commit to paper, finding my experiences and realizations fruitful on their own journeys towards their crown, and mind you, not necessarily a crown of diamonds.

Acknowledgements

I would like to thank my family—my parents, Misha, Anjani, Anant-Vijay and Vikas—for supporting and encouraging an author in the making.

I would like to thank the organizers of the *Femina* Miss India contest for giving me the chance to participate, and be involved in a truly incredible experience.

I would also like to thank Meru, my awesome editor at Penguin, for working on this book with me through its many stages. Professor Marilyn Sides helped me develop my writing skills and looked at the manuscript in its various forms, and always gave me excellent advice.

Most importantly, I would like to thank God for always being there for me. Thank you.

9CCC47 5'215 1/-

Preetam